ALSO BY AMANDA HAMM

By Its Cover

Amanda Hamm

ISBN: 978-1-943598-11-3

By Its Cover is a work of fiction. All names, characters, places, events, etc. are products of the author's imagination or are used fictitiously.

1

Hiding in the shop was a completely rational decision. I saw Eric coming out of a building across the street. I didn't want to talk to Eric. Ducking into the nearest shop before he saw me was the most logical thing I could have done.

I shoved Eric out of my head to check out where I was. Apparently, I'd walked into a store that sold useless fragile stuff. The glass shelves on either side of me were lined with a variety of glass and ceramic items in different sizes. They all looked as though they had been designed to do nothing except sit around on a shelf.

An old woman, maybe seventy or so, with gray hair and a plain pink dress stepped out from behind one of the shelves and greeted me with a smile. "Hello."

"Hi," I said.

"Welcome to Granny's Shelf," she said. "Can I help you with anything?"

"No, thanks." I waved away her help. "I just came in here to avoid someone."

She nodded understandingly. "Feel free to look around until he's gone, dear."

I turned to the nearest shelf, not because I had any interest in the abstract glass or weird green swan, but because I didn't want to acknowledge that she'd correctly guessed the person to be a *he*.

My eyes landed on a very strange object. It looked like a crystal turtle but with miniature peacock feathers. As I leaned closer to investigate, my breath tickled the feathers and made them dance. It was unexpectedly cool, and I felt an impulse to check the price.

I successfully resisted that impulse, probably based in part on my recent training. My head was firmly in charge now. I didn't do things that didn't make logical sense. Something that was nice to look at but served no purpose had no place in my life. This was a principle that I had pretty well figured out. Sometimes the opposite gave me trouble though.

There were things that did serve a purpose that I wanted in my life. The most significant was a guy who could fill the role of husband and father. I tried to find him online. Geography was a hindrance. I lived in the teeny tiny town of Andauk, Ohio. There were a few other towns close enough to consider a match so I included them in my search. The age I left pretty wide.

My search resulted in three guys with excellent potential. I even met all three of them in person, at different times of course. But all three of them had apparently been disappointed in my potential. I didn't renew my membership on the site. I opted to focus on guys who physically crossed my path.

At first, it seemed that God approved of my decision. An announcement appeared in the church bulletin the same week about a new young adult ministry forming. I went to the first meeting. As far as I could determine, there were only two available guys. One was clearly interested in someone else. The other didn't even look at me. And the absence of a wedding ring was my only evidence he was single anyway. I didn't consider that conclusive.

That had been back in August. I'd started going again in November because... Well, I admit Eric had something to do with it. Seeing him there had been an unwelcome surprise indeed. Seeing him getting into his car now as I peeked through the window was a relief. I watched his car pull from the parking spot before I decided the coast was clear.

Before I made it back to the shop door, it flew open in front of me. A gray-haired man wearing a jumble of clothing stepped through it. He seemed to be in a rush and visibly startled at the sight of me. He recovered and bowed deeply in my direction.

I moved backwards. I couldn't help it. It was as though the stench of body odor had hit me in the face. I tried to offer a friendly smile anyway. He probably either couldn't help it or wasn't aware of it. I didn't talk to him though because I was trying not to inhale.

The man might have been bowing to the shelf behind me for as much attention as he paid my response. He faced the old woman at the end of the shelf as soon as he was upright again.

"Morning, Jojo," she said.

He smiled and held his hand out to her, palm up.

I didn't know what he wanted and turned to the old woman to see if it meant something to her.

"You need a shower," she told him, which didn't exactly answer my question.

I felt guilty for being curious, but the man was blocking my exit.

She hadn't answered Jojo's question either because he pushed his hand closer to her with a surprisingly cute pout.

"Shower first," she said sternly.

Jojo nodded and began to unbutton his top shirt. I could tell by the haphazard collars that he was wearing a thick stack of them. It looked odd but made some sense because it was December, and he wasn't wearing a coat.

"Go to the bathroom before you start shedding layers," the woman said, "so I don't have to pick up your trail of laundry."

He nodded seriously and began walking towards the back of the shop. He peeled off two shirts before he made it through the door. Both of them were dropped on the floor where he'd taken them off.

The old woman let out an amused sigh as she turned back to me. "My brother," she said.

My curiosity must have shown on my face. I smiled to acknowledge appreciation for the information that really wasn't any of my business. It was past time to leave. "Thanks for letting me look around," I said as I moved to the door. I saw her bending to pick up the nearer shirt before I got outside.

I gulped in as much fresh air as I could. Unfortunately, the air was right around freezing. I groaned as my lungs burned in response to right around freezing. I noticed Heather had found a better parking spot in front of Joseph's Gym. I ignored the discomfort of breathing to rush across the street to go in with her. She saw me coming and waited.

While I had joined the group at church, St. Jude's, to meet guys, I was at least making friends. Heather hadn't gone into detail, but she'd come right out and told me that she needed new friends because her old ones had recently ejected her from their ranks.

Part of me wondered if I should worry that she had done something to make them turn on her. But a bigger part of me wanted to be her friend because I had some idea how she felt. A woman who had been my best friend for more than ten years cut ties after I made the mistake of breaking up with her brother. Enough time had passed that I could admit my real mistake had been dating him in the first place.

Heather waved when she saw me. "Morning, Julia," she said.

"Good morning," I answered.

She glanced uncertainly at the front door. "Do we knock?"

Joseph's Gym wasn't open yet, not because 10 am was too early but because December was too early. The gym was still two weeks or so from its grand opening. We didn't need to knock though because I saw Emily through the window, and she clearly saw us. She was already hurrying towards the door.

Emily had moved to Andauk only a few months ago. She'd quickly set to work making as many friends as she could. She was a bit flighty – I once caught her talking to a picture on the wall – and sort of a klutz. But I liked her anyway, and it'd been easy to agree to today's favor. Emily was dating Joseph, the one whose name was on the building. He'd apparently talked her into leading a class there, and she wanted a few of us to come over for her to practice.

"Hi!" She smiled brightly as she held the door open for me and Heather to come inside. "Thanks so much for doing this."

I rushed in out of the cold and looked around. The gym was mostly a big open space. It wasn't the kind of gym that had a lot of exercise equipment. It was more like a school gym, ready to be converted for multiple uses. I knew Joseph, or at least recognized him, from the same young adult group at St. Jude's. His broad chest and thick arms made it easy to believe he was a guy who owned a gym. He also had a dark mop of hair and a sweet smile that could fit in with a boy band. Emily hadn't stood a chance.

I tried to warn her that it was a bad idea to date a good-looking guy because it would be too easy to lose her head. But she willingly flung it over her heels within a couple of weeks. Yeah, weeks. That was how quickly nice packaging could do its damage.

He was sitting on the floor by the wall messing with some speakers. The way he kept glancing at Emily made me think he'd been equally overmatched. Perhaps the two of them would end up happy in their joint foolishness. I certainly wished them well.

Joseph's sister Ruth was standing next to him when we came

in. She walked towards the door as I unzipped my coat. She had straight red hair that was very long and looked pretty mashed onto the top of her head. My hair wasn't really straight or curly. It was mostly wavy and whenever I tried a messy-on-purpose bun like Ruth's, I just looked like someone who had lost her brush. I opted for a neat ponytail which I hoped was still neat as I pulled off the headband that had been keeping my ears warm.

Heather's hair was brown like mine and similar in texture. Hers was a bit shorter as it barely brushed her shoulders. She hung her coat on a hook next to mine. When she pulled her hat off, a good portion of her hair lifted from her shoulders into the air.

I couldn't resist a quick laugh.

She immediately started smoothing her hair with both hands.

"Sorry," I said. "I wasn't laughing *at* you."

"I know." She sounded resigned, not hurt. "Hats make me look like I stuck my finger in an outlet." She pulled a rubber band off her wrist to show she was prepared and secured most of her hair with it. A few shorter strands hung loose.

"It looks like you guys are all ready," Emily said. "Can you wait here for a minute, and I'll get ready and come over here like I'm welcoming you to the class?" She turned around with a little skip of enthusiasm, then quickly faced us again. "Oh, and everyone pretend you brought a kid with you."

Heather said, "Huh?"

That pretty much summed up my reaction.

"The class will mostly be parents and children," Emily tried to explain, "so if you imagine you have a kid with you, you can let me know if I'm going too fast or something seems too complicated." She smiled and jogged to where Joseph was sitting.

"I don't think that's going to happen," Heather said.

I didn't say anything, but I'm sure I looked as though I agreed with her. It wasn't unwillingness. I just didn't know much about kids. I could imagine a little girl next to me, but I wouldn't have the faintest idea how she might be perceiving the class. Either of my nieces would probably be having a tantrum by the end regardless of Emily's teaching.

Ruth, who was almost as single as me and Heather – she'd been dating someone for a few months – was just as childless. She shrugged at us. "Well… I guess we'll do the best we can."

I nodded and began to rub my hands together. It had seemed warm when I first came in because it was much warmer than outside. But now that I was standing there in a short-sleeved shirt, it was downright chilly.

Ruth noticed. "My brother is cheap," she said. "He won't heat the place more than necessary. I think he'll crank it up a few degrees once it's open, but he thinks everyone will be moving around enough not to mind a slight chill."

Heather hugged herself with an eye roll.

Ruth was wearing a sweatshirt and her hands were tucked into the ends of her sleeves. She appeared more prepared.

Music blared through the speakers starting in the middle of a song. Then the volume lowered as we all looked that way. Emily came towards us with a big smile. She was wearing a few layers and a headset mic. "Welcome to Joseph's Gym," she said. "Everyone come line up over here." She waved an arm towards the center of the gym. "Pick a dot to stand on."

I saw colorful dots on the floor, spaced out far enough that I could stand on one and wave my arms without hitting the person next to me. The marks seemed like a good idea for grown-ups so they were probably smart for kids, too. I left a red dot open in front of me to my right. That seemed like where I might want to keep an eye on an imaginary child.

A picture on my parents' wall came to mind. It was me at six years old with messy hair and missing front teeth. My future child wouldn't look exactly like me so I changed her eyes from brown to blue. That was a mistake. I gave her lighter hair instead. My brother had been blond as a kid so I could easily imagine that as a family trait. And if Eric had been blond as a kid, I didn't know it. Therefore, it had nothing to do with him.

Heather was next to me and Ruth was on her other side. The whole front row of dots was empty. Their imaginary children were probably standing next to mine.

"Are you having trouble with the music?" Heather asked.

"The speakers are secondhand," Emily said, "and they were shorting out. But I think Joseph has it fixed."

"No, I mean…" Heather pointed, possibly at the sound waves in the air. "Is this the right music?"

I'd been wondering the same thing, in between trying to picture a child. When I thought of ballet, I expected something with a piano or an orchestra. We were listening to guitars and heavy bass.

"Yeah," Emily said. "Remember, it's not a real ballet class. It's just…"

"Inspired," Joseph supplied. He was now standing beside Emily. He had a deep voice that filled the space without a mic. "It's *inspired* by ballet."

I nodded.

Heather nodded.

Ruth waved a hand at her brother and said, "By the way, you can leave now."

"What?" He looked surprised.

Emily gave him an apologetic smile. "We don't really need an audience."

"I was going to help." He gestured somewhere near Ruth, presumably at an empty dot.

"You've seen me practice before, and I thought this might be, you know, just us girls."

"Go on," Ruth said. "Surely there's something in the back that you could, like, inventory or something?"

"Kicked out of my own gym," Joseph said. He shook his head as he began to walk towards the far end. He playfully pushed Ruth's shoulder as he passed her.

"Okay." Emily clapped her hands to bring attention back to her. "Pretend you know nothing about ballet."

That was going to be a lot easier than pretending I had a child.

2

"That was pretty fun," Ruth said.

Heather nodded, looking perhaps a little more surprised than she should have.

"It was," I agreed.

Emily had us skipping around the room and wiggling to the music in dance moves that probably would have looked silly on our own. Somehow, no one looked silly when everyone looked silly. It hadn't been an intense workout but enough that I was warm and had been slightly out of breath in the middle. I didn't want to seem in a hurry to leave, but I kind of wanted to put on my coat while I was warm so I could stay warm.

Emily motioned us towards the coats as though she had the same thought. "Bundle up," she said. "I have a great idea how I can reward you all for your help and give you a chance to give me some detailed feedback at the same time."

I led the charge and Emily explained her idea on the way to the corner. "We'll go to Burger Brothers," she said with a glance at the time. "It's after eleven so Chip will be open. I'll get him to make us his special shakes."

"Oh," Heather groaned with reluctance. "I don't think we burned that many calories."

"No, trust me." Emily became animated and spoke with her hands waving in the air. "He cuts up fruit and just adds skim milk and ice, but he whips it up so frothy it's like you're drinking a real milkshake. But for less than a hundred calories. It's almost like delicious air. It's so good."

I was convinced.

Heather was, too. "I'm in," she said.

"Me, too." Ruth was zipping up her coat.

"Let me just tell Joseph that we're leaving." Emily ran towards the back. She was only gone a minute. As she ran back up to us, Joseph stepped out of a back room long enough to wave.

We hurried down the sidewalk. Burger Brothers was only a few doors down. I knew it was the one with the big, red-striped awning. I also knew Emily worked there. I had never been inside. I didn't think I'd been to any restaurant since my last date, which felt like a long time ago. I didn't want to sit in one alone. Going in with a bunch of friends felt like a great idea though.

Small Christmas trees were lashed to the lampposts we passed. Strings of colorful lights outlined the window on the front of Burger Brothers. The first thing I saw when we went inside was a woman wearing a Santa hat and a dress covered in purple flowers. For a second, I couldn't figure out how she was coming at us so fast. Then I figured out that she was on wheels, lime green roller skates.

"Hi, Emily!" She came to an abrupt stop before crashing into us. She'd clearly had a lot of practice on those skates. Tufts of curly gray-blond hair stuck out under the fur of her hat. "Friends means you're not here to work."

Emily shook her head. "Not yet," she said. "I'm going to get Chip to make us special shakes."

"Oh!" The woman's eyes lit up. "I'm going to watch."

She was excited to watch us order? That seemed weirder than her red, purple and green outfit.

Emily laughed and waved us all forward. There were several

people scattered about in booths and one person at a counter in the back. The man taking his order appeared to be somewhere in his fifties with a thick moustache, a green t-shirt, and a white apron. I guessed, however, that his name was Chip and not Luigi.

Emily turned around before she got to the register. "Who wants strawberry? Who wants banana? And who wants both?"

"Both," I said.

Ruth paused for a moment before she said, "Just strawberry for me."

"What are you getting?" Heather asked.

"Both," Emily said. "I like strawberry, but the banana makes it a bit sweeter."

Heather nodded. "Okay, me, too."

The man in front of us moved off to the side where there was a window for picking up orders.

"Hi, Chip." Emily smiled brightly as she stepped up to the register.

He grunted in response.

"We would like four of your special light shakes," Emily said. "Three with strawberry and banana, one just strawberry."

Chip didn't move a muscle. He stared at her as though he hadn't even heard.

"Please," Emily added.

He continued to stare for a moment, then bent his arm at the elbow with one finger raised.

I followed where he pointed and found a menu hanging from the ceiling. It was a black sign with white letters, almost impossible not to read once I was looking at it. I saw milkshakes but not anything about them being special or light. Banana wasn't even a flavor.

Perhaps I saw what I was supposed to see because Chip eventually said, "That's not on the menu."

"I know." Emily glanced over her shoulder to give the rest of us a reassuring nod. "But you make them so awesome, and I know you have all the ingredients back there."

I looked behind him as she spoke. The kitchen was fully visible through the opening in the wall. I saw the backs of two people who looked like teenagers washing dishes. There was a younger man – younger than Chip but older than the teenagers – slicing tomatoes. He had dark hair and a thick but neatly trimmed beard.

I thought he might be thirtyish. That fit in my age criteria. He was clearly employed, which was also a positive. While he certainly wasn't bad looking, I didn't feel any particular jolt of awareness or attraction when I checked him out. Someone I could consider objectively was at the top of my list. Appearance-wise, he was perfect.

Unfortunately, he was wearing plastic gloves and the angle made it impossible to tell whether or not he was wearing a ring. His eyes lifted. He gave a nod of recognition to Emily.

"Hi, Luke," she said.

He lowered his eyes to his work. But they popped up for one more second to meet mine. Perhaps he was showing some interest, though I couldn't tell if it was me or only why I was staring at him. I turned my attention back to the ordering stalemate.

Chip was glaring at Emily, who seemed to be waiting patiently for something to happen. Ruth was standing right next to Emily at the counter. She took a step backwards to line herself up with me and Heather. Emily offered the three of us a nothing-to-worry-about smile. I was more worried for her because this guy was her boss, and he seemed kind of annoyed with her.

"Um…" Ruth glanced at Chip and then Emily. "Maybe we should…" She tipped her head towards the door.

"Yeah, you guys go ahead and sit down," Emily said. "I'll bring the shakes over." She cracked a brief smile before her face returned to nonchalance. It was enough to make it even more obvious that she knew that wasn't what Ruth had been about to suggest.

Chip let out a sigh so big that if he'd been a cartoon character, his moustache would have danced all over the place. Instead, I felt my eyes dancing around to see if Heather and Ruth were going to take a seat or leave or what. Chip turned around before he'd finished.

"See?" Emily gestured to his retreating back. "I knew he'd do it. He's secretly very excited that I like the shakes enough to bring friends to…" She broke off with a smile as Chip switched on something loud and rumbly that covered her words. The noise stopped after only a few seconds. Emily waved us towards a booth. "Come on. It'll take him a few minutes."

We settled into seats. The booth had a blue cushion on the seat and back with lighter blue stripes. Both were firm and smooth. I'd heard that the restaurant was a fixture in Andauk, which made me assume it had been there way too long for the booth to be original. It must have been replaced recently. I don't think I was the only one wondering if we were going to be waiting a lot more than a few minutes. No one said anything about that, and I was just as interested in some social time anyway.

"Okay, how'd I do?" Emily asked.

"It was great," Heather said.

"It *was* great." Ruth spoke a bit hesitantly. "But if you really want constructive feedback…"

Emily nodded for her to continue.

"The only thing I'd say is that there was a part near the end where you had us doing a lot on one foot. Heather lost her balance a few times, and I was pretty wobbly. I couldn't see Julia."

She paused, but I didn't say anything. I had noticed Heather struggling with her balance, and I wasn't sure it was necessary to point out that I hadn't for whatever suggestion Ruth had to offer.

"That surprised me," Emily said. "I always think of myself as a huge klutz so it never occurred to me I might have better balance than anyone."

"You're supposed to be better because you're the teacher," I said.

"Yeah," Ruth agreed. "I don't even know if kids have better balance than us, and it's not a problem exactly... I just thought that if they're falling a lot that might distract them from paying attention to you."

"Oh." Emily looked thoughtful. "I could see that making people giggly."

"Maybe if you space it out," I suggested.

She squinted in confusion.

"I mean, alternate between the one-foot and two-foot exercises."

Emily still looked confused, but maybe she was only thinking because she nodded like she understood. "I grouped everything to make it easier to remember," she said. "But maybe mixing it around would help keep everyone's attention. Notecards would be better than bored or giggly students."

"Emily!" A woman's voice called the name from somewhere near where we'd ordered.

I couldn't see around the booth, but Emily jumped up and headed that way.

The woman with the Santa hat rolled up to our table a minute later holding a glass in each hand. "Who wanted no bananas?"

Ruth raised her hand.

She set one glass in front of Ruth and the other in front of me. Emily was right behind her with two more glasses.

"You ladies enjoy the treat." The older woman – I guessed her to be around my mom's age – skated backwards as she left. She gave a friendly smile and dodged another table without looking at it.

Emily had returned to her seat and seemed to be watching for our reactions.

"This is really good," Heather said.

I nodded agreement as I tasted mine.

"I can't believe he made you something not on the menu," Ruth said. "I've seen him give people the stink eye just for asking him to leave off the mustard."

"The man is all bark," Emily said. "He wouldn't even let me pay for these."

"Really?" Heather and I asked at the same time. Ruth was taking a sip, but her eyes widened with the same question.

Emily smiled at the surprise. "He tried to give me a hard time about how he couldn't charge me because Beethoven – that's what he calls the register – doesn't have a button for things people aren't supposed to order. Don't worry though. I won't make this," she waved a hand over our drinks, "a habit. I wouldn't want to take advantage. Or test the limits of his secret niceness."

I thought about secret niceness while I enjoyed a cold and delicious drink. Cold was an odd choice for December, but delicious was always a good choice. Was secret niceness anything like not letting your right hand know what your left was doing? Or did the mean front undo the backstage good?

Ruth caught my attention with a tiny gasp. She was looking away from all of us and seemed to make up her mind before she reached her hand into the air and waved.

I turned to follow her gaze. She appeared to be waving at a

young man who shared her red hair and freckles. I wasn't sure he was her target because he looked right at her, then deliberately kept walking towards the counter.

Ruth put her arm down and whispered, "My brother," which only explained the part of the situation that I'd already guessed. She rolled her eyes slightly at his lack of reaction. It didn't cover the hurt he caused.

Meanwhile, Heather had quickly wrapped one arm around her head and turned inward. She was obviously trying to hide her very red face. I wanted to know what was going on but felt that all these friends were too new for me to start probing them with personal questions. I poked my drink with my straw and hoped they would fill me in without me having to ask.

"Still getting the full-on silent treatment?" Emily asked gently.

Ruth nodded. "I don't know what she told him or..." She stopped and looked at me. "That's my brother, Adam, who just came in. He broke up with his girlfriend about three weeks ago. They were together more than three years so he's taking it understandably hard. But he's also taking it out on the family." She sighed and lowered her voice further. "I don't know if she blamed us when she dumped him or what. There was never any open hostility, but from the first time he introduced Kayla things were tense. It was just clear that she didn't really fit in with... Maybe we could have tried harder, but she didn't make us want to. Anyway, Adam hasn't spoken to any of us since she left him."

I tried to make my nod sympathetic. I'm afraid I couldn't stop looking at Heather though. I was really curious about her embarrassment. I think it was my constant glances that made Ruth finally notice that something was wrong.

She leaned towards Heather and hissed, "Do you know something?"

Heather shook her head with a miserable expression. She was still trying to blend in with the back of the booth. "Kayla blamed me," she said softly.

"You?" Ruth looked surprised. And wary. "Why?"

"Can we wait until he leaves?" Heather begged.

She was mostly talking to Ruth. Emily and I looked at each other. She appeared about as clueless as I felt. There were a few pieces I could place. Kayla was evidently the name of Adam's recent ex. Since Heather knew Kayla, and that Kayla blamed her for the breakup, it seemed reasonable to assume it was related to Heather seeking out new friends.

We went back to chatting about Emily's ballet-like class for a minute, distractedly. The backs of the booths were high enough that I couldn't see what was going on in a lot of the restaurant, but I did see Adam's back as he walked the other way carrying a bag in one hand and a drink in the other.

I might have suspected that Heather asked to talk about it later in the hope Ruth would forget if she hadn't been the one to restart the topic. She glanced around the booth shortly after I saw Adam walk past and then gave Ruth a quick nod.

Ruth simply raised her eyebrows and said, "So?"

"I didn't do anything, I swear." Heather looked at me and Emily. "Kayla and I were friends since like sometime in Jr. High. Us and these two other girls. We got together all the time. When Kayla started dating Adam, she didn't ditch us. She just started bringing him along. The more time I spent with him, the more I realized..." Heather put her hand on her forehead and focused her eyes on the table. "I realized I was falling for him," she mumbled. She looked up again and kept talking as her face grew redder. "Nothing happened and nothing was going to happen. I would never... and Adam would never... But it was awkward to be around him when I was feeling things I shouldn't so I tried to see Kayla and the others only when Adam wasn't going to be there."

Heather took a breath and stirred her straw around. "It mostly worked for... I don't know, a long time. But every time I thought I was over the crush, I'd accidentally bump into him or something and realize I needed more time. A couple months ago, Kayla figured out that I was avoiding him. She kept asking me why I didn't like Adam and what did I have against him and... I kept saying nothing and she kept not believing me and... She was relentless, just would not let it go. I finally told her the truth. I thought she took it well. She said she was actually relieved that not *everyone* was against them. Sorry, Ruth."

Ruth shrugged. "Despite our issues, I am genuinely sorry for both of them that the relationship ended badly."

"Me, too," Heather said. "I did not..." She sighed again. "Anyway, a few days after I told Kayla, she called me. She was really upset, said she had to break up with Adam because she'd never be able to trust him now that she knew someone was waiting in the wings for him, which I wasn't. She said it was all my fault and that I should have kept my feelings to myself, which I tried to do. I reminded her that she was the one who wouldn't stop bugging me and accusing me of hiding something. It got ugly. She was screaming at me and I know I said things I shouldn't have, but the way she was talking made me scared... I thought she was going to tell everyone, including Adam, that she was breaking up with him because of me. If people heard her blaming me, they would assume that I..." She bit the side of her lip against what she didn't want to say.

It didn't matter. We had the general idea where the sentence was going and the conclusions people would draw if another woman's name was associated with a breakup.

"The conversation was so heated, we both knew it was the end of the friendship," Heather continued sadly. "Our other friends sided with her rather than try to navigate in the middle. I don't entirely blame them, but it still sucks."

I felt myself nodding along with Emily and Ruth.

"I should not have admitted anything to Kayla," Heather said. "I should have kept my mouth shut no matter how many times she asked."

"Well..." Ruth seemed to be considering her words. "Regardless of whatever... I don't think you can blame yourself even if Kayla does. It sounds to me like she was looking for an excuse and you just gave her one. I would never consider someone else's feelings evidence that Gabriel might cheat on me."

"Me neither," Emily said. "If, let's say Julia, said she had a thing for Joseph, I'd be like, 'Fine, we'll get together when he's not around until you find your own man.' Honestly, it sounds kind of weird that she had Adam tagging along with her friends all the time."

"Maybe," Heather said. She put on a falsely bright expression. "But I can't change the past, and at least now I get to do fake ballet with you guys."

"That's right, silver lining." Emily gestured to the table. "And you get to experience healthy milkshakes."

I didn't correct her. She could call it a milkshake if she wanted. It was super tasty even if it wasn't much like a milkshake.

"Hey, speaking of new friends and dropping the subject," Heather said, "why didn't Ella come today?"

"I tried to talk her into it," Ruth said. "But she just wasn't comfortable dancing in front of people."

"That big front window makes me a bit nervous, too," Emily said.

"It was probably just us that —"

Heather's mumbling was cut off when Ruth said, "Oh! Now

that we're actually speaking of Ella... A few days ago, she got a Christmas card from a secret admirer." She grinned broadly at this news.

Emily let out a quiet squeal.

Heather gasped.

I just tried not to roll my eyes.

"Was it just unsigned," Heather asked, "or did it actually say from your secret admirer?"

Ruth had a straw in her mouth, but she pushed it away quickly and said, "Neither. It said... I'm not going to remember the exact wording, but it was something like, 'Someone who doesn't know you well but knows enough to wish you weren't out of reach wants to wish you all kinds of happiness this Christmas.'"

"Oh, that is interesting," Heather said.

"It's sweet," Emily said.

I kept quiet. But dangerous was the word I would have used. Ella had better be careful not to be taken in by some romantic nonsense.

"I wonder who sent it," Heather said, looking thoughtful.

"Ella doesn't know?" Emily asked.

Ruth shook her head. "No return address, but the postmark was local."

"She doesn't even have a guess?" Emily sounded skeptical.

Ruth seemed to pick up on that. "Why do you ask like *you* have a guess?"

"Well, I thought, um..." Emily spoke slowly. "I probably shouldn't say what I think if Ella hasn't considered it."

"No, I think you should say." Ruth leaned forward eagerly.

Emily winced as though considering, then shook her head. "No. No, I better not. If I'm wrong, I might end up embarrassing someone."

"Who?" Heather asked.

"Ella, most likely," Emily said.

"Oh." Ruth sat back looking resigned. "You're probably right. But you are new in town. You can't know that many people. I'm going to be paying attention to see if I can see what you see."

3

I rolled the cart outside first thing Monday morning. It was the one thing I needed to do before we officially opened, and I liked to do it before I'd hung up my coat anyway. I had the key to the book drop and the front door with my personal keys. It made me feel kind of important to hold the keys when I'd only worked at the library for a year.

But only if I didn't think about it too much. Lillian had given me the keys on my first day. I soon learned that it had little to do with my trustworthy appearance and more to do with her not being a morning person. I spent the first part of each day by myself. Well, by myself except for all the patrons, most of whom preferred the self-checkout. I rarely interacted with them beyond waves and basic greetings.

I piled all the books from the box into my cart and pushed it back inside. I scanned all the books before I lined them up on a wheeled shelf for volunteers to put away later. It wasn't exactly exercise, but it was enough for me to warm up. When I returned from hanging my coat in the back room, the big clock read 8:58. There was already someone standing outside the door though so I used my awesome authority to unlock it early.

Mornings at the library had a mix of young and old. Most of the people I saw were retirees or toddlers with their moms or dads. Sometimes it was a retiree with a toddler. The young outweighed the old as typical of Mondays because it was a storytime day. Lillian hadn't been late for storytime yet. She did like to make me sweat though.

It started at 10:30. If Lillian wasn't there by 10:00, I'd start looking over her planned books. At least twice, she'd walked in the door just as I resigned myself to filling in for her. That Monday wasn't quite another example, but she gave herself only a few minutes to spare.

"Morning, Julia," she said as she breezed past me to put away her coat and purse.

"Good morning, Lillian."

She came back to the desk surveying the library with a practiced eye. Her gaze took in the big clock, to which she nodded and said, "Just in time." She picked up the books and walked towards the storytime room with confidence.

I didn't know how long she'd been doing storytime, but I knew she'd been at the library for twenty-two years. Perhaps it was how long she'd been there and perhaps it was just her nature, but Lillian was an easygoing boss. She had an answer for everything and never seemed frazzled. It was a small library in a small town. She could probably run the place by herself. Some days, it seemed that all I did was check in books and answer the phone to tell people our hours. But I was the backup. I needed to know everything Lillian did to cover the earliest part of the day and in case she needed a day off, which hadn't happened since I started.

Most of our volunteers were high school students looking to earn community service hours for confirmation or school or some club. Eric had earned his confirmation hours at the library. That's why he thought of it when he was looking for something other than work and sleep to fill his days.

That's what he told me anyway. I didn't believe him. I mean, the part about doing nothing but working and sleeping before. We talked many times, and he'd admitted that he also ate. And visited his parents. And went to church. And watched football and hockey. Among other things.

He didn't have a predictable pattern for showing up at the library. I put one cart of books back, hidden from the volunteers who came right after school, so there would be something for Eric to do if he came. I needn't have worried because the only teen I saw was Sami, and she was later than usual.

Sami was a seventeen-year-old ball of energy who bounced through the doors clutching a phone in one hand and keys in the other. Both items clinked against the counter as she put her hands there and said, "Hello!"

"Hi, Sami," I said. "Are you here to put away books or just to check some out?"

"Oh, I'm volunteering," she said. "My mom wanted me to pick up my brother from school and drop him at soccer practice first because she's not feeling well. My dad will get him from soccer so I can stay a whole hour. Is it okay that I'm late? Did someone else reshelve all the books already?"

"Plenty for you to do," I assured her, motioning her to follow me. I hadn't intended to grill her about being later than usual. I pulled two little carts of books forward. "We have lots of kids' books. Do you want fiction or nonfiction?"

She grabbed the closer cart and said, "I better work on fiction. I'm much better with the alphabet than all those... numbers and stuff."

I nodded. Numbers were easier though, at least backwards. When I returned to the front desk, I saw Sami's keys sitting there. That was not remotely surprising. I rolled my eyes before I returned them to her. She stayed a little over an hour. Lillian was chatting with her so I heard their occasional laughter from children's nonfiction, where she'd moved eventually.

Sami pushed an empty cart towards the desk when she was ready to go. "Oh!" she said. "I just realized I forgot my form. Will you guys remember I was here today if I have you sign it next time I come?"

"Of course, honey," Lillian said.

I smiled. I knew we'd remember. I wasn't sure Sami would. I glanced at her hands to make sure she had both items she came in with. Sami might not have been even five feet tall and Lillian only had two inches on her. At only five foot five myself, it was unusual for me to find myself the tallest person in a room. I experienced a weird moment of towering over them. It was as brief as it was weird as the door slid open nearby, and I sensed a taller person entering.

It was Eric. He was the last person I wanted to see, and yet my heart buzzed with excitement at the sight of him. The guy was making everything difficult.

"Hi, Julia," he said. "Do you have anything for me to do today?"

"Definitely. I think the usual kids are all getting busy with Christmas stuff." I made a move to bring him the fuller cart.

He rushed past me to take it before I could. "I'll get right to work then." He waved at Lillian and Sami. "Good afternoon."

He'd barely disappeared behind a shelf when Sami leaned closer and whispered, "Who's that?"

"Just another volunteer," I said. "His name is Eric Chadwick."

Lillian was coughing behind me. I glanced back, but she seemed okay. She actually seemed to be smiling through the cough.

"He's cute," Sami said. "Maybe he's really here to see you."

"He's here to shelve books."

"If you say so." Sami took a step towards the door, stopped to retrieve her phone from the desk, then continued out the front door.

I checked the computer to see if we had any hold requests. Nothing since the last time I'd checked. Probably the most pressing task was to shelve some books. It'd be more efficient for me to work in a different section. But I *could* help Eric. I could also slam my hand in the drawer under the desk, and that would be about as smart. I was kind of torn between the two bad ideas.

"Why don't you go help Eric?" Lillian suggested.

"Okay," I said. She was my boss after all. If I put up any resistance, it might become a big deal. Helping Eric didn't have to be a big deal. I followed him into adult fiction and found him staring at the D section.

He looked up at me and smiled. "You're so far behind that you need to help?"

"Well, we know how slow you are," I teased.

He laughed and handed me the book he was holding before he picked up another one. "So, uh... What are your plans for Christmas?" he asked.

"Nothing much," I said. "Of course I'll go to church, probably Christmas Eve, then I'll spend a couple of hours at my parents' house."

"Huron, right?"

"Yep."

"Your brother coming?"

"Yep."

Eric slid a book onto the shelf. "My brother is younger than me and doesn't have kids," he said. "It's pretty quiet at our parents' house. Do your brother's kids make Christmas more exciting? The present part?"

"I wish."

Eric looked a bit startled by my tone.

The truth, however, was that my brother's two girls were the primary reason I was not looking forward to Christmas.

He looked at me sideways as I reached around to grab another book. "Do you want to vent about what makes you sound grumpy or do you want to tell me to mind my own business?"

"I suppose if I didn't want to talk about it, I shouldn't have sounded grumpy," I said. Although I no longer felt grumpy after he looked at me like he was more afraid of being told to mind his own business than of hearing a long, drawn-out rant.

"That's true," he said. "It was a cry for permission to vent, which I grant."

"Well… what is the diplomatic way of saying that my nieces are little brats?"

"Sausages?"

"Huh?"

Eric winced. "Sorry, terrible joke. Brats as in bratwurst."

I laughed once I got it. "They aren't always sausages, but more and more it gets really uncomfortable when it seems that neither my brother or his wife have any idea how to… I don't want to say control, but…"

"Give me an example," he said. "Paint a picture."

"Okay." I looked into my memory even though I knew we were about to pay even less attention to the books. "The last time we were all together, about six or eight weeks ago, my mom called everyone to the table for dinner. I was braiding some doll's hair for Abigail, she's four, and I put in a rubber band and she came right to the table with me. But the older girl, Jessilynn, was playing on a tablet and didn't want to put it down. She's almost seven, by the way. Her mom, Lauren, went over and asked her all politely if she'd put down the toy for dinner. Jessilynn flatly refused. So then Lauren crouched down next to her and asked again. She was almost pleading, and Jessilynn just completely ignored her. It was really awkward with the rest of us sitting at the table waiting and trying to pretend we couldn't hear. Then Lauren snapped and took away the tablet. She told Jessilynn she could have it back after we ate. Jessilynn did not take that well. She began shrieking, 'Give it back!' over and over and over and just threw a total fit."

"I'm guessing that did not improve the awkward level," Eric said. He looked sympathetic, and as though he actually cared what happened next. Or at least cared what I was going to say about it.

"Depends what you mean by improve," I said, "because it definitely increased. I could see my mom twitching, like she desperately wanted to intervene but didn't want to be the intervening mother-in-law."

Eric smiled. "My mom was just telling Ruth that when she marries Gabriel, she should call her Mom 2 instead of mother-in-law because of the stereotypes."

"Are they engaged?" I asked. I'd thought Ruth had said she and Gabe had only been dating a few months.

"Not officially." Eric shrugged. "But they've known each other forever. We all know they'll end up married before long."

"Oh." I nodded because it sounded as though they'd been friends for a long time first, and I approved of that. I hoped Eric remembered how I approved of that. He'd been helping at the library since August. He'd been standing next to a back-to-school poster the first time I talked to him, and I hated that I remembered that. After several visits, I'd become afraid that he was thinking about asking me out. I casually slipped into the conversation that I thought it was important for two people to be friends for a while before they started dating. And in hindsight, I knew it hadn't come out all that casually. Eric had seemed to understand perfectly why I'd mentioned it. He boldly asked how long a while was.

Months. At least. That's what I'd told him. It hadn't been subtle at all, but it bought me some time.

Eric pushed the cart farther along the shelf so we could continue the charade. "So did you guys ever get to eat dinner?"

"Uh, yeah." It took me a few moments to figure out where I was in the story because thinking about Eric asking me out was a huge distraction and apparently thinking about him *not* asking me out was little better. "After Jessilynn shrieked for – well, it was probably no more than a few minutes, but it felt like forever – Lauren started trying to bargain with her, saying she could play with it as soon as dinner was over and if she calmed down, she could even have it during dessert. Eventually, she just gave up and set the tablet on the table. We ate the cold food with cartoon noises in the background and otherwise tense silence."

"If that wasn't an unusual scene," Eric said, "I can see why you might not be super excited to spend Christmas with them."

"They're my family so it still sounds terrible to say," I said. I kept my eyes on the letters in front of me to actually get a book on the shelf while I conveniently avoided eye contact with Eric as well.

"No, it doesn't." He sounded thoughtful.

I wondered what sort of justification he might come up with, but something made me think he believed it.

He said, "It sounds like you want to see your family even though it isn't always pleasant. That isn't terrible. It's just a difficult situation."

"Thank you," I said, which felt wrong. What was I thanking him for? For understanding me? For having eyes so strikingly blue, I couldn't help staring? Oh, man. We were stuck in a really nice, awful moment. Someone needed to say something.

Eric lowered his eyes to the spine of the book in his hands.

I wanted to thank him for that. Fortunately, I managed to resist that impulse.

He moved to the other side of the cart to shelve a book, then he picked up another one. "How would you spend Christmas in an ideal world?" he asked.

In an ideal world, I'd have a husband to lean on when other family was difficult. I'd always pictured myself married by the time I was twenty-six. But that was not an ideal I had any intention of sharing with Eric. Best to stick to my present reality. "Well, I'd go to Midnight Mass, then sleep in. What time is it?"

Eric pulled a phone partway from his pocket and said, "About 5:30."

"No, I mean, Midnight Mass." I moved to Andauk in February so this would be my first Christmas at St. Jude's.

Eric was looking at me with a lot of uncertainty in those blue eyes. "Are you seriously asking me what time *Midnight* Mass is?"

"That's not a stupid question," I insisted. "The pastor at my old church scheduled Midnight Mass for 10 PM because he didn't want to stay up so late."

Eric smiled. "Okay, I'm sorry for judging you without all the facts. It's actually midnight here. How late would you sleep in?"

"Not crazy late," I said. "It's just that my parents expect me to be at their house by eight so they don't have to hold the girls off opening presents too long. I'd rather get up without an alarm, have a relaxing breakfast, maybe listen to some Christmas music, then go to my parents' house in time for lunch."

"Do you like traditional carols or..." Eric raised his eyebrows, waiting for me to fill in the blank with what I liked.

"I love it when modern bands make the traditional lyrics rock. My mom says that ruins them, but..." I shrugged. There was nothing wrong with having different taste in music than my mom.

Eric nodded. "And then?"

"Well, I'd spend a few hours with my family, during which nobody had a tantrum and everybody got along. Then I'd come back home for a quiet evening." I tried to picture that quiet evening and how I'd be most content spending it by myself. I would not be completely alone though. "Snowflake would curl up on the couch next to me, and she'd be purring of course. I'd be rereading a big stack of Christmas cards even though I didn't send many of them."

Eric interrupted again with a confused expression. "Do you normally send yourself Christmas cards?"

"No… I meant… I only exchange cards with a handful of older relatives. If we're talking ideal, I'd get a card from everyone I know regardless of how many I sent out. Speaking of Christmas cards…" Oh, no. Was I really going to bring that up in front of Eric? "I was talking to a friend the other day about someone who got a Christmas card from a secret admirer. That's stupid, don't you think?" Apparently, I wasn't just bringing it up, I was asking his opinion. That was worse.

It appeared Eric didn't know what his opinion was. He considered for a moment before he turned it back to me. "*Is* it stupid?" he asked.

"Well, yeah. The whole point of dating someone is to get to know him, to find out if you have enough in common to spend a life together. It's pretty hard to get to know someone if he won't even tell you who he is."

Eric nodded, slowly, like maybe he wasn't fully convinced. And he smiled a little, like maybe he was amused by my argument.

I was blushing. Completely out of nowhere, I felt my face heating up at the topic I should have avoided. I needed to get away from Eric. "I think I'm slowing you down," I said as I scooped a handful of books from the lower shelf. Those came later in the alphabet and therefore belonged in different aisles. I gave a quick nod as I left him. I hoped it conveyed that I was simply trying to do my job and not running away from the feelings he provoked.

4

Eric came to help at the library again on Friday. I did not talk to him while he was putting away books. I'd like to say this was because of an improvement in self-control, but that might be lying. Okay, it would be lying.

A kid came in about the same time as Eric and asked me to help him find books on a particular subject for school. The kid rejected many of my suggestions, and I didn't finish with him until Eric was leaving. He told me he was looking forward to seeing me later at the young adult meeting at church. The library closed at six, which gave me two hours to eat dinner, get ready for the meeting, and convince myself that I was not looking forward to seeing him.

St. Jude's was a fairly small church, which made sense given the size of the town. There was an elementary school behind it. Our meetings were held in the teachers lounge. Eric wasn't there when I entered.

I noticed that mostly because Gabriel was the first person I saw, folding up a table. He looked a lot like his brother so it made sense that he would make me think of Eric. Neither was overly tall, but Gabriel was taller and skinnier. Though maybe being skinnier just made him seem taller. I'd never measured. They had the same bright blue eyes. Gabriel turned his to me and said, "Good evening, Julia."

I said, "Hi." I don't think he heard because for some reason, his greeting made Ruth kick him. It was only a gentle, playful tap with her foot.

She said, "We're not doing that."

"All I said was good evening."

Ruth put her hands on her hips. "No, you said good evening."

She may have pronounced the words a bit slower, but I did not understand the distinction.

I looked at Ella. She gave me a small smile before she turned back to organizing chairs for the meeting.

"Good evening," Gabriel said again.

I turned to see who he was addressing as Ruth repeated, "We're not doing that."

The newcomer was Isaac. He laughed at his sister because he apparently knew what she was talking about. I was curious, but I was more curious about the people with Isaac, his wife and newborn daughter. I rushed over to peek into the car seat as Jessica set it down.

"Aw." She was so tiny. I'd seen Grace for the first time the previous Friday, and she still wasn't quite a month old.

Jessica smiled proudly.

"You look great," I said. Then I realized that I sounded surprised that she looked great. "I mean, you don't look horribly sleep-deprived. Is she sleeping pretty well?"

"Not at night," Jessica said. "But she naps a lot so I've been getting naps, too, and it's not so bad."

I wanted to ask if I could hold her, but Jessica had seemed pretty possessive the last time. I might need to wait until she was a little older, or at least a time when she wasn't sleeping so peacefully.

"Just checking to see if she's still cute," a masculine voice said over my shoulder. "She is."

It was Sebastian Jones. The guy was already on my radar as a dating prospect. Liking babies was another point in the pro column.

"Hi, Sebastian," Jessica said. "I hear you brought more food while I was asleep the other day. Thank you."

He cooked, too?

Sebastian acknowledged the gratitude with a smile. "Isaac told me how he tried to help."

Jessica rolled her eyes. "I don't know how a person burns noodles. I just don't."

The others were listening and there was quite a bit of laughter. "How *did* you do that?" Ruth asked.

"I fell asleep," Isaac said. "The baby is waking me up several times a night, too."

"Oh, no. Look at that sweet, sweet face." Ruth pointed at the sleeping newborn. "Is that really who you want to blame for your incompetence?"

"You need an extruder," Gabriel said.

He and Ruth seemed like a good match because I was not understanding either one of them that night.

Isaac shrugged. "I'm just saying what happened. I don't think making it more complicated would have helped."

"It would have kept you awake." Gabriel claimed a chair as he spoke.

The rest of us took the cue to begin filling in the circle. Emily and Joseph always came in late together, and I figured they'd want to sit together. I sat next to Sebastian to leave two empty chairs between me and Gabriel. I surreptitiously studied his profile while he chatted with Isaac. Sebastian was a decent-looking guy. Dark hair and eyes, only a few years older than me.

I tried to tell myself that looks wouldn't matter at all if I was doing this self-match-making thing objectively. But I could objectively tell myself that it would be a bad idea to marry someone I found physically repulsive. What he looked like mattered a little.

Sebastian lived with his mom. At first, I thought that might be a red flag. I had since gathered that she was significantly older than my parents, and that it was more appropriate to say she lived with him. I could respect a caretaker.

Sean came in just as my thoughts turned to him as another option. I still knew very little about him. He was kind of short for a guy – probably not more than an inch or two taller than I was – and he was overweight. The glasses were the biggest turnoff though.

Glasses in general were not a problem. Gabriel wore weird old-fashioned glasses, but they looked really good on him. They drew attention to the vivid blue they framed and somehow fit his personality. What was an extruder and how did it keep someone awake? I wasn't sure I wanted to know. And Ella had several different pairs of glasses that were all pretty. She swapped them out like jewelry. Sean's glasses, on the other hand, didn't seem to fit his face. They were slightly tinted and hid his eyes, or at least obscured them.

He did have a few points in his favor though. Showing up at the young adult group was something we had in common. The fact that he rarely spoke up in meetings was the reason I knew next to nothing about him. It also meant that he might be someone with whom I could enjoy some comfortable silence.

It hadn't taken me more than a minute to process all these thoughts about Sebastian and Sean. That was all I was allowed because Eric was the next person to walk through the door. He waved a hand as various people called out greetings. I thought he was approaching the chair next to me, but then he veered off to sit between Sean and Jessica. It was possible that he realized those empty chairs were the only adjacent ones and saved them for the late couple as I had. It was also possible he wanted a peek at the baby he was now sitting near.

I watched him across the circle as he smiled at the car seat. Something inside me went mushy for a moment at his reaction to the newborn. It made me turn away quickly. I found Ruth staring at me. "Who are we talking about today?" I asked her.

"Since this is the last meeting before Christmas," she said, "we want to start with St. Wenceslas."

"Wenceslas?" I said. "Is that the good king in the song?"

"Exactly," Ruth said.

"Actually…" Gabriel glanced at the clock. "It's nearly time to start. Could you all look up the lyrics to the song as we're getting ready? I have a couple paper copies if anyone has trouble finding it or just prefers to read on paper."

I was vaguely aware of Sebastian getting up to grab one of those paper copies as I typed Good King Wenceslas into my phone. I looked up when he didn't come directly back to his chair.

Heather had arrived. Sebastian had stopped to let her cross in front of him to the chair on my other side. She kept her eyes on him as she sat, though her head was turned away. I'd seen her look at him like that before, like she was afraid of him. And not the way I was afraid of Eric. There was something going on there that I needed to ask someone about before I had any serious designs on Sebastian.

Gabriel led us in an opening prayer just as I found the song lyrics. Then he gave us a few minutes to read the story in the song.

"Um, I have a question," Heather said. "I thought this was a Christmas song, but it doesn't actually mention Christmas. Is it a Christmas song just because it mentions snow?"

"No." Ruth shook her head. "The first line says it happened on the Feast of Stephen. St. Stephen's Day is December 26th so it happened during the Christmas season."

"Oh." Heather looked back at her phone.

I was reading the last verse when she spoke into the quiet again.

"Is this even English?" she asked. "Because I don't think I get it."

"It's English from a few hundred years ago," Gabriel said. He sounded thrilled.

Ruth put a hand on his in an apparent attempt to restrain the enthusiasm. "It was written a long time ago, and Gabriel loves that. He was talking like someone from the Middle Ages the whole time we were working on this week's questions, and it was really annoying."

Gabriel grinned as though he was proud of being really annoying.

"Okay." Heather drew out the word like an audible eye roll. "'In his Master's steps he trod, where the snow lay dinted,'" she quoted. "What does that mean?"

"He walked behind the king," Gabriel said. "In his footprints. The story says that heat actually came out of the footprints to keep him from getting frostbite or even freezing to death on his way to aid the poor man."

"And that's where we want to start," Ruth said. "Sort of. Right after that it has the line about whoever blesses the poor will find blessings. So we –"

"Ye," Gabriel interrupted. "It says ye who shall bless the poor."

Ruth sighed. "Yeah. The question is… Can you think of a time when you received an unexpected blessing from helping someone else? And not just the satisfaction of helping?"

I thought of something right away, but I wasn't sure it was quite what she meant. After a minute of no one else saying anything, I decided to share my example.

"Well…" I paused as people turned to look at me. "When I was ten years old, our next-door-neighbors asked me to watch their cat for two weeks while the family was out of town. I went over every day to feed it and clean the litter box and stuff. It turned out my parents wanted to use it as a test. I'd been bugging them to get a cat for a long time, and they wanted to see if I still wanted one after I had a better idea what was involved. I did. We got a cat. Unfortunately, we lost her after six years. But then we got another one, and I still have her. She's definitely a blessing in my life."

I saw a few smiles and nods. There was probably at least one dog person in the room, but I sensed general approval.

"This is…" Isaac stopped and gave Sebastian a strange look. He seemed to be asking for permission to say something.

Sebastian just shrugged at him.

"Well, um, Sebastian and I became friends through some pickup basketball at the park," Isaac said. "I have to admit that at the time, I thought I was being generous to include him. But then he helped me get a much better job than the one that I hated and… Well, I quickly figured out that I wasn't the generous one."

"Not the good-looking one either," Joseph said as he came into the room, which was great timing. It kept the moment from becoming overly sentimental.

Isaac gave his brother a punch in the arm as he took the seat next to him.

Emily hurried across to sit on the other side of Heather. "Sorry to interrupt," she said. "Where are we?"

Gabriel got to recite a few of his favorite lyrics to catch her up. Then Jessica explained how she became friends with a coworker after she helped her jump-start a car with a dead battery. Joseph observed that making friends through acts of kindness was wonderful but shouldn't be unexpected.

That was when I accidentally made eye contact with Eric. He had met me when he volunteered at the library. Was he thinking about that as a surprise blessing? Why was I thinking that? And why was I letting my heart flutter even the tiniest bit? My head put a stop to that nonsense.

I gladly looked towards Ruth as she moved our discussion along. We talked about St. Stephen, the first martyr, and the tone became more academic as we read his story from Acts of the Apostles. I enjoyed that part of the meeting and was sad to see it end, mostly because we had to skip the next two Fridays for holidays I was doing almost nothing to celebrate.

Our group rearranged the furniture for the meetings and was expected to put it all back when we were finished. It appeared that Ella and Sebastian were staying to help the leaders so I slipped out with the others. Maybe I was making excuses, but it really seemed that more than four people would just be in the way.

Heather walked out with me. She seemed to move at a deliberately slow pace to make space between us and those ahead of us. I matched her speed. She glanced over her shoulder before she whispered, "Sometimes I still can't believe Sebastian Jones has the nerve to show up here."

I was pretty sure I looked as startled as I felt. "What makes you say that?"

"Oh, that's right," she said. "You're not from here."

I shook my head to confirm what I didn't believe she'd honestly forgotten.

"Don't buy the nice guy act." She looked over her shoulder again. "It's an act."

I wasn't sure what to say. I wanted to know what she was talking about. But it felt very wrong to talk about someone I'd just been talking to, especially when Heather seemed eager to tell me and no one else.

Heather made it easy for me, in a way, by not waiting for me to ask. "I don't know how he got Isaac to vouch for him, but everyone likes Isaac and that's the only reason Sebastian hasn't been kicked out. He has a serious violent streak." She lowered her voice further and quit walking altogether. "He dated this girl named Kathy when they were in high school. Right after graduation, she tried to break up with him, and he got so mad he broke her arm, her collarbone *and* one of the bones in her face."

"Oh, my goodness!" I barely breathed the words because now I didn't want to be overheard either.

"That was only the first time. There was another girl when he was in college. They say she was in the hospital for a week. There've been at least two others he's beaten up since. One was from Sandusky and the other...uh..." Heather seemed to give up trying to remember the location. "The act is good though. He goes to church every Sunday, helps out his mom, seems just as polite as can be... That's why women keep falling for him. Of course, the eyes don't hurt. The guy has really nice eyes. He looks at you like he's a little worried you might be afraid of him, and even knowing why you *should* be afraid doesn't make it less attractive." She looked back and motioned for me to start walking again. The noises of moving furniture had stopped.

Joseph and Emily were standing outside the door when we left the building. It was dark and cold, but the house closest to the church had decorations that made me stop for a moment. Every window had a lighted wreath and the porch and front bushes were thoroughly covered.

"Too cold to stand around," Heather said. "Bye, guys." She moved swiftly towards her car.

I was about to make a similar exit when Emily said, "Julia, do you want to get together sometime this week? Since the whole group isn't meeting?"

"Um... okay."

"I usually spend Sunday afternoon with the Zieberts." She gestured to Joseph because that was his family name. "Are you doing anything Saturday?"

"I have to work Saturdays," I said.

"Oh, right." She bit the side of her lip and thought. "What day do you have off?"

"Wednesday."

"Perfect. I don't work until three so you can come over for lunch and we can, uh..."

"Braid each other's hair?" I suggested sarcastically.

She laughed. "Well, we'll talk and... the Zieberts have a lot of games. If I remember, I'll borrow something while I'm there."

"Sure. That sounds good," I said, and I meant it. I'd been starting to feel a bit lonely again. That was part of the reason Eric seemed so dangerous.

5

Monday was kind of a repeat of the previous Monday. Sami bounced through the front door and plunked her keys and phone on the desk in front of me. "Guess what! Guess what!" she said, her eyes bugging out.

"What?" I asked.

"My painting will be in the first batch of eye exercise!"

"What?" I repeated myself because she told me, and I still couldn't guess.

She tried to rein in her smile long enough to explain. "You know the new place opening downtown, Joseph's Gym?"

"Yeah. I've been inside."

"Really? Is it nice?"

I nodded. I didn't think I could get as excited as she was about a gym – or anything else – but I had enjoyed Emily's practice class and everything inside looked very new.

"Well, the owner, Mr. Ziebert, is letting the art classes have some wall space to display our work in public." Sami put everything down to clap her hands together. "My painting is gonna be in the first batch when it opens next month. I just found out today."

"Congratulations," I said. "I'll have to get Mr. Ziebert" – it felt weird to call Joseph that – "to let me in to see it."

Sami just stood there grinning at me while she went up and

down on her toes. Then she said, "Books!" and pointed at some carts behind me.

"Help yourself," I said.

Her eyes got round as I motioned her behind the desk so I pushed the cart enough to meet her halfway.

Lillian came up behind me a moment later and asked, "Did she say eye exercise?"

"Yes."

"Did she make that up or...?"

I didn't know so I shrugged. "I'll ask Emily next time I see her."

Lillian looked confused before she nodded. I supposed it took her a few seconds to make the connection from Emily to Joseph to the gym. But she said, "When you said Emily, I thought you were about to say Eric."

"Why would Eric know anything about the art at the gym?"

"I don't know that he would," Lillian said. "I just thought that's what you were going to say." She smiled innocently.

I chose not to fall into her trap. The woman was always trying to get me to talk about Eric so she could make insinuations. Even her youngest child was a few years older than me. I guess that might have been why she felt entitled to engage in motherly snooping. There was nothing to snoop out though. I responded by narrowing my eyes in a way that I hope told her it was strange for her to suddenly be thinking about Eric when I certainly wasn't.

He sort of ruined it by entering the library and walking towards us.

"Hello, Eric." Lillian greeted him in a tone that threatened to tell him we were just talking about him when *we* were not talking about him. Only Lillian was.

I mentally kicked her.

"Hi, Mrs. Bentley. Hi, Julia." He seemed unaware of the suspicious tone or the imaginary retaliation. He nodded to a Christmas countdown on an easel by the door. "Nice wreath," he said. "Who drew it?"

I pointed at Lillian. "She did. I can't draw a stick person."

"I don't believe you," Eric said. He looked at Lillian before I could respond. "I do like the wreath though. Very festive."

"Thank you. Festive is exactly what I was going for," Lillian said. "Should I have Julia put you to work?"

Eric smiled at both of us. "That's why I'm here."

"Okay. There you go." I pointed at the nearest cart.

"There you go?" he said. "I guess the pleasantries are over."

I smiled but fought against laughing out loud. I didn't want Lillian to get any ideas about me enjoying Eric's company. At least not any more than any other volunteer.

He seemed satisfied to have made me smile – a thought that would unsettle me if I let it – and took the books towards juvenile nonfiction.

Lillian did me the favor of waiting a few minutes before she suggested I could help him. "We're caught up otherwise," she said.

"Then I will check for misfires," I said.

She smiled knowingly. "In juvenile nonfiction?"

"No," I said, and I headed a completely different direction.

Misfires were what Lillian called it when patrons thought they were putting books back where they got them and missed. When there was nothing else to do, we'd scan the shelves for these out-of-order books. I had thought it would be a terribly boring part of the job. But I'd also thought misfires would be rare. I found some every time I checked, and it was oddly satisfying, like pulling weeds might be satisfying to a gardener. There were usually more in the children's sections. I headed for early readers.

A nice side effect was that I couldn't think about anything or anyone else while saying the alphabet in my head over and over. I found three misfires right away on the first shelf. There was one on the next as well. I became engrossed in the job and honestly forgot I had an ulterior motive for starting it. Until I found a Z in the Ns. I was squatting at the end of a row. I yanked the book and stood up just as someone else came around the corner.

"Hi," I said, but not really. I made a squeaky startled noise and tried to tack something that sounded like hi on the end of it.

Eric had also jumped. He paused a moment to let us both recover. "Sorry," he said. "I found this phone on the floor. Do you have a lost and found box or something?"

"No need," I told him because I recognized the glittery purple case. "That's Sami's." I reached out and took it from him.

He touched me.

It wasn't fair to accuse him when I was the one who grabbed the phone. But when our hands touched, he made me feel unwanted warmth and sparkles. My only recourse was to pretend it didn't happen. "Thanks," I said. "I'll give it to her."

He nodded. Then he stood there a moment before he turned around. It seemed he was going to say something else but either changed his mind or couldn't think of anything to draw out the exchange. I found the proper place for the book in my hand before I hunted Sami.

She was almost finished with the cart when I spotted her. I held the phone behind my back and said, "Hey, Sami, are you missing anything?"

Her hand froze as she was about to take a book. Her mouth dropped open and her eyes darted around, possibly searching some internal checklist. Then her hand flew to her back pocket. "My phone!"

I smiled and held it out to her.

"Thank you," she said as she took it. "I swear I would have realized I didn't have it before I left." She sounded more concerned about someone giving her a hard time for losing it than about actually losing it.

"It looks like you're almost done." I nodded at the cart. "We can call it an hour when you finish that even if it isn't quite an hour."

"Great! Thanks." Sami reached for a book.

She called me back before I'd made it more than a few paces. "Hey, wait, um... Wait."

I noticed that she never called me by name. I thought maybe my age made it awkward. Maybe I was too old to be Julia and too young to be Miss Dierksheide. And maybe she just didn't remember my last name. I didn't mind regardless of the reason. I just turned around.

She was unfolding a piece of paper. "Can you sign my form now, while I'm thinking of it?"

"Sure. Be right back." I took her paper to the front desk to find a pen. I was only verifying that the kids showed up when they said they did, but I felt like I had real, grown-up authority when I put my signature on a school form.

I passed Eric after I gave it back to her.

"Still checking for misfires?" he asked.

I stopped and looked over his shoulder. "Do I need to check your work?"

"What? I am awesome at this."

"Really?" I asked. "Do you brag to everyone about your counting skills?"

"Only the people I want to impress." He was obviously kidding about the counting skills. There was something in his eyes that hinted at a sincere desire to impress me though.

I wanted to continue the teasing without acknowledging the other part. I wanted to talk to him without sounding like I was flirting. I wanted to run away, and I wanted to stay close. I put on a serious expression and said, "I better check." Then I moved past him so that we'd be working on the same shelf but not too close.

I focused on the numbers in front of me even though I remained aware of Eric's nearness as I followed him. We worked side by side in silence for a few minutes. It was comforting to feel his presence and not be worried about what to say or how it might sound. But eventually I realized that I'd caught up to Eric. He was just standing there, watching me.

I tilted my head to ask what he thought he was watching.

He opened his mouth, closed it, then opened it again. "I'm trying to decide if I should be offended that you are actually checking my work."

"Not just your work," I said with a wave at the shelf. "Lots of people have been over here today."

"Hmm." He frowned, looking as though he didn't believe me. The disgruntled expression disappeared suddenly as he seemed to get an idea. He reached across himself to pull a book from the top shelf then – without taking those bright blue eyes off me – he stuck it onto a lower shelf.

I felt my eyes widen in surprise.

He kept watching me as he pulled out another book and put it where it didn't belong.

"What are you doing?" I asked.

He shrugged nonchalantly and moved the cart to the other side of the aisle.

I figured out what he was doing. He was giving me something to do, giving me a reason to stay right there next to him. I kind of wanted to strangle him and hug him. I settled for imagining that I'd knocked him in the back of the head with the first book I pulled out.

"Julia?"

"Yeah?"

Eric was quiet so long I thought he forgot he was going to ask me something. Then he said, "What are you looking for?"

I was looking for the other book he'd moved. We both knew that, and that's how I knew that wasn't what he was asking. "What do you mean?"

"You said… you said before that you wanted to be friends with someone before…"

He didn't need to finish the sentence for me to see the direction the conversation was headed. I felt a bit unsteady and sat down on the floor to stare at the books on the bottom shelf.

"What do you want that friendship to look like," he said eventually, "to know it's worth… pursuing?"

That was a reasonable question. I tried to take a few calming breaths while I figured out a reasonable answer. "I guess I'm looking for a lot of things."

"Can you be more specific?"

I almost laughed at the way he sounded overwhelmed by the response. Did he really expect me to give him the key to a great relationship in a few words? But I nodded slowly.

Eric lowered himself to the floor a few feet away from me, still holding the book he'd been about to reshelve. He seemed to be preparing for a longer answer.

What I really wanted was to be comfortable enough with a guy that I could tell, objectively, with my mind, that he was a good fit for me. I didn't want any distracting infatuation. It would be difficult to articulate that to Eric without implying that I found him very distracting. I tried to explain without getting into that.

"I guess I'm looking... I'm looking to know someone well enough that there aren't any surprises after we're already attached. I want to be able to talk about important things like kids and money before I'm invested in the relationship. I don't want to be tempted to stay in a bad relationship when I find out six months in that he's gonna expect me to take the kids to church by myself every Sunday while he stays home to mow the lawn just because breaking up is hard."

Eric nodded like he understood. In fact, he nodded like he respected and agreed with my reasoning. That was terrifying. Mostly because I was afraid he was going to start asking me about all those important things right there on the pebbly hard carpet of the library. He evidently thought we should put aside the heavy topics. "What do you do for exercise?" he asked instead. "Or do you exercise?"

I shook my head. "Nothing consistently. I keep thinking I should get some good habits while I'm still young and healthy, but... sometimes I walk in place while I watch TV."

"That's something," Eric said encouragingly. "Have you ever taken any martial arts classes?"

"No."

"Joseph wants me to... Let me back up." He waved his hand as though pushing his thoughts back. "I've known the Zieberts a long time. Adam and I were in the same class and we were good friends all through school until... well, we kind of drifted apart after high school, but... anyway, you know Joseph is about to open his gym?"

I nodded.

"He wants to start up a hapkido club there and –"

"Hapkido?"

"It's a form of martial arts."

"Okay," I said.

"So he wants me to join so not everyone is starting at the very beginning." Eric sighed. "I'm not sure I wouldn't be starting at the beginning. I only made it to a blue belt, and I quit when I was, um... fourteen. But I've been thinking about it just because it would be some regular physical activity, which I could probably use."

"Do you think it would be fun?" I asked. "Because I think that's what would help me, if I found something fun."

"Oh, yeah." He nodded enthusiastically. "It's controlled fighting. Punching, kicking, knocking each other to the ground... all without actually getting hurt. Most of the time."

I laughed because the 'most of the time' sounded the most appealing to him. But then I laughed because I realized that he'd been talking to Joseph. "Wait," I said. "Do you actually know something about the art in the gym?"

"The art?" He wrinkled his forehead in confusion.

Clearly, he did not know about the art or what I was talking about. "Never mind," I said. "You're joining the martial arts class then?"

"Well... my concern is... Joseph's trying to make it a family place, get people to bring their kids. Would it be weird if I was the only guy who didn't have a kid with me?"

My first thought was that Joseph didn't have any kids so I pointed that out.

"That's true." Eric looked surprised he hadn't thought of that. "Where did you work before you came to the library?"

Oh, boy. Loaded question. It didn't have to be though, only if he asked why I left. "I worked in accounting, accounts payable specifically, at some big company."

"Really?"

"Why does that shock you?"

He shrugged. "Not shocking exactly. It's just... now you're surrounded by books. It seems like you went from math to English."

"Hello." I pointed at the books behind me. "Dewey decimals, remember?"

"I know," he said. "And for the record, I have mastered the order of those numbers."

"Yes, we've established your awesome ability to count."

"And we've established that you doubt that ability." Eric sounded disgusted, but I knew it was in fun.

I shook my head as though doubting couldn't be helped. "You give me reason when you are so careless as to misfire on purpose."

"It worked," he said.

It was still working. Fortunately, he didn't give me time to dwell on that.

"Do you like working here?" he asked. "Aside from when people misfire on purpose."

"I do." I smiled because I'd lucked into a dream job without even knowing what my dream job was. "It's quiet and calm, but not boring. Just peaceful. Lillian's a great boss, even though now and then she stresses me out when I think I might have to do storytime. But otherwise —"

"You don't do storytime? I thought..." Eric tipped his head to study me. "I've gotten the impression that you like kids and you like books so... What's wrong with storytime?"

"Nothing." I braced myself to admit something embarrassing. "I'd love to do storytime, but... Lillian is *really* good at it. She does these cartoony voices that crack the kids up, and she dances and... I think the kids would boo me off the stage if I tried to take her place."

Eric looked sympathetic but also dangerously thoughtful. "Maybe you need to practice to boost your confidence," he said.

"And I happen to have a book right here." He held up the book he'd been flipping around in his lap since we sat down.

"That is a book about eating your vegetables," I said. "There is a reason we don't do nonfiction at storytime."

"You get better at something by challenging yourself. If you can make the story of vegetables entertaining, you will be ready to rock storytime."

"Except that is not a story." I pointed at the book that looked dry even for nonfiction. And, yes, I was totally judging it by its cover.

"Oh, yeah?" Eric opened the book with a defiant attitude. "Once upon a time, there was a... what is that? Oh, it's a carrot. Once there was a carrot, and it said, 'I have lots of vitamin A!'" He cleared his throat and continued in a falsetto. "Now I'll introduce you to my friend the..." Eric turned the page and squinted at it.

I was curious about the quality of those illustrations.

"The green bean," Eric continued. "Hello. You want to eat me because..."

His green bean voice sounded exactly the same as his carrot voice, and I was laughing too hard to pay attention to its lesson.

Eric stopped and looked at me silently until I quit laughing at him.

"No offense," I said, "but that was awful."

"You can't make calling me awful not offensive just by tacking 'no offense' onto it."

"I didn't say you were awful. I said your story was awful." I closed the book before he could try to read what the next vegetable might say. "I think you proved my point about nonfiction being bad for storytime."

"No way," Eric said. "I proved *my* point that you need to practice. That was what it sounds like when someone doesn't practice."

I was still amused by the performance. "Just out of curiosity, why are all the vegetables girls?"

"They were just supposed to sound like little kids."

"Oh."

Lillian appeared at the end of the aisle. "Sorry to interrupt," she said, "but you two do know that it's time to go home, right?"

I did not know that. I checked the time while Eric jumped to his feet. It was a few minutes after six. I scrambled to my feet before I realized Eric had held out a hand to help me. I was glad I hadn't noticed.

"I'll get out of your way," he said. "Bye, Julia. Have a good night, Mrs. Bentley."

I pulled out that other book Eric moved before I forgot about it. Then Lillian and I managed to lock up without her making any comments about me sitting down on the job. She seemed happy about the situation, and I almost wished she would have yelled at me for shirking.

My drive home was barely five minutes. I'd worked at the library a few months before I moved to Andauk. The super short commute was only one reason I was still glad I'd made the move. My old place was in the middle of a large apartment building with thin walls. Now I rented a little house all by myself.

Well, by myself with Snowflake. As I walked up the sidewalk, she streaked from out of nowhere to meet me on the porch. I usually came home for lunch and let her outside for the afternoon. The cat we'd had when I was younger used to leave "presents" for us when she spent time outside. I was grateful Snowflake didn't do that. It allowed me to imagine her out frolicking with other animals rather than hunting them.

I grabbed my mail from the box. I loved that it came right to my door and not a mail center half a block away. Snowflake had her face against the door while I unlocked it. I liked to think she was racing inside to get the place ready for me. Really she probably thought it her right as supreme being to enter first.

The mail appeared to be two advertisements and two Christmas cards. I set it on the table to check out more closely after I was comfortable. I hung up my coat, got a plate of food together, then dumped something into Snowflake's dish. I was right about the ads. I set those aside for the recycling bin.

One of the card envelopes had my aunt and uncle's return address so Christmas greetings seemed a strong guess. The other one didn't have a return address. I figured it was going to be a fake card, something with generic holiday sentiments sent from a local business to get me to visit. But it had been addressed by hand with my name even spelled correctly so someone at least put some effort into disappointing me.

My aunt and uncle included a short note about some travel they'd done recently. Snowflake was already done eating and rubbing her face against my legs. I reached down and stroked her soft fur. Then I opened the last piece of mail. It had a simple nativity silhouette on the cover, simple but pretty. It was a real card. The printed text inside read, "Wishing you joy and peace this Christmas."

That was also simple but pretty. I didn't really get to enjoy it though. My eyes had already taken in what was written underneath that. The handwritten message wasn't simple. I didn't know what it was. And yet I did. It said, "*Is it still stupid if you know who it is? From a not-so-secret admirer.*"

6

Emily greeted me with a big smile and a wave to come inside quickly. I shivered while she gave me a very brief tour of her very small place. She told me I should just hang my coat on the back of a chair when I was ready to lose it. She had made a couple turkey sandwiches and popped them into the oven to warm up for us.

I shed my coat while she brought a box to the table. It was a game called Loaded Questions. I raised an eyebrow at her.

"Don't worry," she said. "We're not really gonna play. It needs more than two people." She took the lid off the box and pulled out a stack of cards. "Most of the questions are pretty tame like how organized you'd say you are or your favorite ice cream flavor. In the real game, you're supposed to guess who gave which answer. I thought we could just read some questions and see which ones give us something to talk about. And we'll skip any we don't like."

I nodded and took a seat. "That might be fun."

"I hope so," Emily said. "Joseph and I have done this several times to get to know each other. Something tells me it will be different with another woman."

"Different how?"

She shrugged. "More talking I hope. Joseph's like... answer, next question... answer, next question... like it's some kind of competition to see how many cards we can get through."

"Okay." I smiled at her imitation though I couldn't promise I wouldn't do the same.

She picked up the top card. "This one asks us to name something we do every day."

I thought of a few obvious things right away.

Emily apparently did as well. "But let's not say anything like eat or sleep. Let's reword this to ask something you do every day that you think not everyone does."

I was willing to play along. "Well, I don't do it every day, but I have a prayer journal that I write in most nights."

"Cool," Emily said. "I've always liked the idea of journaling, and I think I have at least three of them, but they all have things written on only a few pages. I don't seem to have the discipline to make it a habit."

"Maybe it's not discipline you lack so much as desire," I said. "Not everyone enjoys journaling."

She smiled. "It does sound better to say it's not my thing than to say I'm too lazy, but... I don't know."

"What about you?" I asked. "What's your every day thing?"

"Well... this comes to mind because it's a relatively new habit. I step on a scale every day." She rushed into explaining regardless of whether I was going to ask. "One day, um, several months ago now, I jumped on a scale at my dad's office. You know he's a doctor, right? Everyone gets weighed in. Weighing myself was just a whim, and I was shocked to see that I weighed twenty pounds more than I thought I did. It wasn't the number so much as the fact that I'd been paying so little attention to myself. Because once I knew I'd gained weight, I realized how many pairs of pants I had shoved to the back of the closet because I couldn't button them and how many other pieces of clothing had gotten uncomfortable and how I somehow never made the connection that my body had changed. It was a wake-up call that I needed to be more... purposeful in my life, in my decisions."

"That's... impressive." I was impressed anyway. "I think some people would have just gotten depressed about the extra weight and eaten some ice cream. But you... I don't know how to say it... sort of I guess saw the bigger picture."

Emily smiled modestly. "Sort of. Maybe. I am definitely still a work in progress though. Next question?"

"Shoot."

"Do you have a birthmark?" she asked.

"Not that I know of."

Emily put a finger on her forehead. "I used to have a light strawberry one here. You can see it in baby pictures, but it faded."

A timer beeped.

Emily shoved the card stack at me. "You pick a question while I get our lunch."

I started reading the cards. Some of the questions were terrible. Some I didn't know how to answer. I got fairly absorbed in reading them because I soon realized there was a sandwich on a plate in front of me, and Emily was back in her chair wearing an expectant expression.

"Oh. Um... there's a question here that asks what was the happiest age of your life. My answer would be that I hope that's not past tense. I hope I have a lot more happy times to look forward to."

Emily nodded at me. "Yeah. I definitely hope I have happier times than middle school and... I suppose we could interpret it as the happiest age so far but..." She waved her hand dismissively.

I moved on to another card. "Can you think of something you always wanted as a kid but never got?"

"Um... siblings." Emily paused. "Maybe. I know I sometimes wished I had siblings, but I sometimes thought they'd just be people for me to fight with so I can't say I *always* wanted them. But I usually did."

"Hmm..." Nothing immediately came to mind. "I'm thinking about how much I wanted a cat, but I eventually got one. Something I didn't get. Oh! This is silly, but our neighbors had a trampoline, and I begged my parents for one. They insisted it would be too dangerous, said I'd break a bone by the end of the summer."

Emily laughed. "I know I would have. I'm generally the least coordinated person in the room."

"You did great teaching the ballet class."

"Thank you. But you know I've been practicing a lot, and I am barely recovered from my last accident."

I wasn't sure how to acknowledge her recent limping without calling her a klutz so I steered us another direction. "Speaking of your class at the gym, or of the gym, one of the kids who volunteers at the library is excited to have some of her artwork on display there. Is Joseph hanging art?"

Emily had taken a bite while I was talking and nodded as she finished chewing. "The art teacher approached him about a rotating display of high school students' work. He thought community involvement could be good for business."

"Is he actually calling it eye exercise?"

She choked on her next bite. When she finished coughing, she said, "I can't believe that's caught on. I said it when he told me about the idea. I was joking, and now he has everyone calling it that."

Emily let me eat for a minute before she asked for another question. The sandwich was tasty.

"What was the last book you read?"

"Hmm..." She winced. "I'm afraid it's been a while since I read a whole book. I've been reading snippets from the Bible most recently, but I don't think that counts. It might not be the last one, but I remember reading *Emma* not too long… Oh, it's been at least a year now that I think about it."

"Jane Austen?"

Emily nodded. "I've still never read *Pride and Prejudice*. I guess I'm working my way onto the bandwagon very slowly. What was your last book?"

I was not going to admit to the very last book. I'd brought something home from the children's nonfiction section to practice reading aloud. It was too embarrassing to say I'd read something about the Declaration of Independence to my cat in squeaky voices. Also, Snowflake had crawled under the couch in the middle of my performance. We were going to talk about the second to last book I finished. "*21 Undeniable Secrets of Marriage*," I said.

"That sounds like nonfiction."

"Yeah."

"If you're reading about marriage, that must mean you're preparing for it?" Emily raised her eyebrows hopefully.

"Someday," I said.

She grinned. "Does that mean we can talk about guys?"

"Okay."

"Yay! I don't want to be pushy if you're not looking right now for whatever reason, but there are a couple of single guys in our Friday night group. I wondered if you have thoughts on any of them."

"I'm trying to form thoughts," I said. "But I'm starting to think I'll need to ask someone out and spend one-on-one time to get to know him."

Emily looked disappointed. "So no one has really jumped out at you?"

"Well, no. I wouldn't want to jump into anything. I'm trying to be smart and practical and… That's why I've been reading marriage books. It wasn't the last one but I think the one before that where it talked about a big survey. When younger people – like under forty I think – were asked why they chose their spouses, they gave answers that sounded like 'he completes me' or 'I couldn't imagine my life without her.' But older people said things like 'she went to the same church' or 'I knew he came from a good family.' The book's author was making the argument that part of the reason for high divorce rates is that people, not all people but enough, enter marriage with ridiculous – and kind of selfish – expectations. They want to be swept off their feet and continue being swept off their feet for fifty years. That's not realistic. I'm trying to be realistic. I don't want fluff. I simply want a guy who values the things I value and wants to work towards a similar future together."

Emily's eyes gradually widened during my speech.

I did not like the strange way she was looking at me. "What?" I asked.

"It's not bad," she said. "I just… I can't believe how much you sound like my dad."

"I sound like your dad?"

"Yes. He was always encouraging me to use my head in a search for a husband. He was like 'Make sure you don't fall for some guy who's all form and no function.'"

The phrasing made me chuckle. "All form and no function? I've never heard a person described that way."

She lifted one shoulder. "He meant… well, he meant to kept an eye on the big picture. It would be bad to marry a guy who's fun to hang out with in the short term but would eventually balk at having our kids baptized."

I was so grateful that Emily didn't laugh at me wanting to be practical about dating. It wasn't until she didn't laugh that I realized how worried I was that she would.

"So let's get specific." Emily leaned closer. "Which guys are single, and who would you try to find out more about?"

"I guess it's between Sean and Sebastian right now," I said. "I've heard really good and really bad things about Sebastian so I don't know what to make of him."

"Yeah." Emily spoke slowly, thoughtfully. I got the impression she was trying to decide whether or not to say what she wanted to say. "I think… maybe you don't want to focus too much energy on him."

Had she heard some of the things Heather told me? I didn't want to gossip, but I wanted to know the truth. "Why not?" I asked.

"I could be wrong," Emily said, "but I think… I think he might be sort of spoken for. Or he's spoken of… someone. But not literally."

"Are you trying to say you think he likes someone else?"

Emily laughed and rolled her eyes at herself. "Yes. That would have been a much easier way to say it."

"Okay. Well, that leaves Sean. I don't remember him really saying anything about himself."

"You might have to go for that one-on-one thing," Emily said. "Have you ever asked anyone out?"

"No. I think I can do it. Especially if I'm not… you know, emotionally invested."

She nodded. "There's another possibility. Maybe."

Oh, no. I hoped she wasn't going to suggest Eric.

"Did you happen to notice the guy I work with?" She waved her hand in front of her chin. "The guy with the thick beard."

"I think so. In the kitchen?"

"Yeah. His name is Luke Wasserman. He's Chip's nephew. I don't… well, he did ask me about you after we all came in for milkshakes." She quickly added, "It might not mean anything. I couldn't tell if he was interested or just saw someone he didn't recognize in a small town."

"Right. I guess if things don't work out with Sean, maybe I'll come up with excuses to visit you at work for some fact-finding."

Emily seemed very entertained by that idea. Then her eyes lit up with another one. "Hey, wait! What about Eric? He's single."

I just shook my head. Eric was out of the question.

"He seems nice," Emily said. "Did you learn something about him that rules him out?"

I shook my head again.

"Then what's wrong with him?"

She may not have laughed before, but she would definitely laugh now. I took a deep breath and told her anyway. "I can't date Eric because I like him too much."

Emily didn't laugh. She sat back in her chair looking incredibly confused. She repeated me slowly. "You can't date him because you like him? What am I missing that that makes sense to you?"

"I don't really like him because I don't know him well enough. I mean… more like a crush." It was awful. I was getting a little warm just thinking about him. "He comes into the library sometimes, and I get stupid. The first time he came in, I picked up some random books and pretended I had somewhere to take them just so I could walk past where he was. Sometimes he says things that aren't funny, and I laugh anyway. He shows up, and I forget that I'm a grown-up with a job. A guy who makes me stupid is trouble. I'll… end up repeating past mistakes."

Emily had laughed at me picking up random books, but she got serious at the end. "Past mistakes," she said. "That's the piece I'm missing, but I won't pry if you don't want to talk about it."

I did. I suddenly wanted to talk about things I'd never told anyone. "I'll tell you, but… I'm afraid I'd have to start way back and make it a really long story."

"I love stories." Emily propped her chin on her hand to get comfortable. "And I promise to keep anything you tell me between us."

I hadn't even thought to ask that. Emily would be a good confidant. "I mentioned that I've been reading books on marriage. I, uh, I started after a painful breakup. Sort of. After I recovered and started thinking about trying again, I decided to invest time analyzing what went wrong. I think I need to tell you how I ended up with Kurt in the first place."

Emily nodded. "Start wherever you like."

"It starts with Sara. She was my best friend all through middle school and high school. We even chose a college together. Sara had a twin brother named Brian. Sometime near the end of our first year of college, Sara asked me if I would be willing to go out with Brian because he was crazy about me. Those were her words. I was so flattered by it that I agreed even though I already knew... I'd spent enough time around Brian to be at least pretty sure we weren't a good idea. But I..."

Emily gave me a sympathetic smile that encouraged me to keep going.

"We dated about three or four months. It wouldn't have even been that long except that Sara was usually with us. It was like I was hanging out with Sara and Brian was just there. Whenever it was only the two of us... we just didn't click. It seemed clear to me we were headed in different directions. Anyway, I eventually told Brian that I thought we weren't clicking. He seemed to understand. Honestly, I thought we both handled it very maturely. But the next time I called Sara, she was ticked off. She told me that if her brother wasn't good enough for me, then I wasn't good enough for her. That was... it was the last time I ever spoke to her."

"Ouch!" Emily said. "Years of friendship just like that?"

"Yeah." I shrugged. It'd been long enough that it didn't hurt anymore. "It didn't seem like her, and now I wonder if something else was going on. I must have caught her at a really bad time and… Anyway, it happened the way it happened."

"I'm still sorry."

"Thank you," I said. "So without Sara, I didn't really have any friends. It sounds kind of pathetic. But I've always been an introvert, not someone who needs a big entourage. Sara was enough. There were still some people I talked to in classes and stuff, just no one I talked to about important things. I mean, other than God of course."

"You're not close with your family?"

"Not really. I like my parents, but I don't consider them friends. My brother is almost five years older than me. We mostly get along but have never been close."

"I can understand that," Emily said. "There's probably a limit to what you can talk about with a brother anyway."

I nodded because she was probably right. Then I kept going. I needed to get through the story while I was still in the mood to tell it and while Emily was still in the mood to listen. "I started working at this big company after I graduated. There were a ton of people around, but most of them were a lot older than me and didn't have much in common with me. I think despite all the people, I was growing incredibly lonely without realizing it. I think that's important. That's why I'm telling you all this backstory."

"Oh, backstory is vital." She nodded. "Plus, all this sharing is good for us."

Emily's eagerness made her seem more like an entourage sort of person. We didn't need to have everything in common though. I appreciated the way she didn't seem to be looking for juicy details. It was more that she cared about my thoughts on the events. It was an awful story, but getting it out was even more of a relief than I expected.

"This is the part where I started noticing Kurt," I said. "He was a coworker. Only a few years older than me and stupid cute. He asked me out, and I wanted him to like me so bad. I didn't spend any time trying to find out if *I* liked *him*. I just went along with everything and tried to avoid any and all disagreements. We were together about a year and a half when he said he wanted... He was on his way to pick up a pizza and come to my place and he mentioned that he wanted to talk about something important that night. I was sure he was going to ask me to marry him."

Emily let out a nervous breath. She could already tell that wasn't what happened.

"He asked me to move in with him instead. I don't intend to move in with a guy until we're married. Aside from... well, I read something a while back that really resonated with me. Of course different people have different reasons for moving in together, but this article said the worst reason was if you're not sure yet if you want to get married, to test the waters so to speak. The point was that moving in together makes it a *lot* harder to break up and the last thing you want to do if you're not sure about someone is make it harder to break up with him because you might end up marrying someone you're not sure about just because it's easier than breaking up."

"Joseph and I have talked about that." Emily was nodding at me. "He said something similar, that inching towards something lets you slide into it. Better to make a deliberate leap."

"You guys are already talking about... leaping?" They hadn't been dating very long at all.

She smiled at my surprise. "Just talking about it," she said. "It's very *practical* to make sure we have the same eventual goal in mind."

I smiled at her use of my word. And I had to admit that not talking was a huge part of why my story was so sad.

"So... Kurt asked you to move in and..." Emily motioned for me to continue.

"Right. The subject had come up before, but this time he said he was officially asking. I'd been wishy-washy when he'd mentioned it but with an 'official' invitation I had to say I didn't think it was a good idea. He was shocked. He launched into a speech about how I was old enough to make my own decisions and couldn't live my life afraid of what my parents might think."

"Your parents?"

"Ah," I said. "You're paying more attention than he was. I hadn't said anything about my parents. They're nominally Catholic at best. They tease me about being practically a nun because I go to church every Sunday. I honestly don't think they'd care if I moved in with him. And that's when it hit me that he was arguing against a reason I hadn't given. I was about to explain my actual reason when he said he hoped we could get married one day, but he didn't think he could marry anyone until he tried living with her. That's when something else important hit me. He wanted to do what I didn't want to do for the exact reason I didn't want to do it. I asked myself why I was sure I wanted to marry this guy who wasn't sure about me. The only reason I could come up with was that I didn't want to break up with him. I was doing it without even moving in, I was wanting to marry him just to avoid breaking up. I started asking him a bunch of questions about kids and faith and... things that are important to me that I'd mentioned but never as though they were important to me. I'm afraid I got totally hysterical." I winced at the memory.

"We broke up that night because I finally understood that the only thing he really liked about me was the fact that I was a doormat. I didn't want to be a doormat anymore. There were a ton of regrets to go along with the broken heart. Plus, I still had to see him at work. We were in different departments so it wasn't like every day, but it was enough. I found out he was dating another coworker not even a few weeks after we broke up. I hoped a change of scenery would help me so I looked for a new job. It was a long time before I landed the position at the library here though."

"You weren't kidding when you said it was a painful breakup." Emily took both our empty plates to the sink. She was studying me with compassion as she came back. "You seem mostly at peace with it now. How'd you get through it?"

"Time mostly. And God. I think it made my faith stronger to know I had a clean slate with God. I focused the prayer journal on how not to repeat the same mistakes. Eventually I felt that I missed having someone in my life more than I missed Kurt specifically. That's when I decided I was ready to try again. But I'm going to be so much smarter this time. And I think that's where we started."

"Right," Emily said, "with Sean as the most practical place to start."

I agreed with her even though I'd been thinking we started with Eric as the least practical place to start.

Emily looked amused. I guessed she knew I was still thinking about Eric. But she picked up a card from the table and said, "All that from 'What was the last book you read?' I knew there would be more talking this time."

7

Christmas, for better or worse, passed essentially as I predicted. The Mass, at midnight, was solemn yet joyous. There were a ton of candles and familiar songs. I spotted Eric across the church sitting with two people I assumed were his parents. He was ahead of me so I could sneak lots of peeks without too much concern that he'd catch me.

I also saw Luke from Burger Brothers. He was wearing jeans and a plain t-shirt. That was disappointing because I liked when guys dressed up for church. It wasn't a deal-breaker by any means so I could still keep him on the back burner. Based on current progress with Sean – over a month and I hadn't even learned his last name – that back burner was way back.

Eric was wearing a suit with a bow tie that matched his eyes. It had the potential to make me consider something as stupid as crossing to the exit nowhere near my car just for a chance to say hello to him. I mustered enough self-control to turn away. That happy decision caused me to bump into Emily. We spoke only long enough to wish each other a merry Christmas.

It wasn't a white Christmas. We'd had at least two good snowfalls, but warmer days had melted everything by mid-December. Now it was just cold again without the white. The lights I passed seemed to twinkle in the super stillness of the late hour. I only had one string wrapped around my own porch railing because I didn't feel artistic enough to create a more elaborate display. It was welcoming though.

My bed was even more welcoming. I felt at peace as I drifted to sleep. Unfortunately, I felt as though I'd barely closed my eyes when the alarm rudely blared in my ear. I dragged myself out of bed to get ready for the day.

Everyone was completely out of sorts when I arrived at my parents' house. My brother and his family had spent the night. His girls had apparently gotten up before the adults and opened all the presents. *All* the presents, not just the ones for them, though most had been for them.

My mom was still clearing away the mess of shredded paper. Lauren was sitting in a corner looking as though she'd been crying and might start again. My dad and brother were talking about work and trying to pretend nothing was wrong and maybe that it wasn't a holiday at all, though I heard the tension in their voices. At least a dozen unwrapped though still packaged toys sat ignored on the floor while the girls played on their tablets with the sound obnoxiously loud. The beeps and pings didn't cover all the sniffling.

My mom was an excellent cook so the food at least was good. We managed some polite though stilted conversation. I didn't stay long after lunch.

The presents I brought were still in a box by the door because no one was in the mood. My mom handed me a sweater and a pair of earrings before I left. There was a gift card from my brother and his wife tucked into the sweater. My best and worst present was still taped to my wall at home, that Christmas card from Eric.

All of my Christmas cards were taped to the wall as decorations. The one from Eric did not have a particular place of honor. If I was being honest, I'd probably reread his the most though. Actually, if I was being honest, I knew I'd reread his the most even though I didn't need to look at it to remember the exact words. His question about if it was still stupid made it jokey and not sappy. That helped me believe it was meant in a joking, friendly way. That was all.

I had to go back to work the day after Christmas, but the library was very quiet even for a library. I mostly chatted with Lillian about her Christmas. Lots of grandkids had visited. She was horrified by the picture I painted of my parents' house. She hoped it was something we could all eventually laugh about.

Snowflake zipped onto the porch as usual when I got home. She was a wonderful companion. There was only one thing in the mailbox so it got my full attention. It was a standard white envelope with Julia Dierksheide written in handwriting I'd seen before. There was no return address. I stood there dumbfounded for so long that Snowflake meowed with impatience.

I unlocked the door for her and followed her inside. I was absolutely bursting with curiosity and ripped open the envelope before I even put my keys back in my bag. It was a single sheet of paper.

1 - I like to make lists, especially if I can cross things off later. I'm not suggesting you cross this off.

2 - I'm allergic to strawberries. It's not serious, just annoying.

3 - People have accused me of being cheap, but I'm willing to spend money on things that are important to me. My favorite charity feeds children at school to encourage them to attend.

4 - I do not understand the success of Oreos. Those are not real cookies.

5 - I root for the Blue Jackets over the Red Wings. No apologies.

6 – _I like math puzzles._
7 – _I think storytime needs sock puppets._
8 – _I have never read Harry Potter._
9 – _I was an altar server for several years and once dropped the bells. Certain people have never let me forget it._
10 – _I used to hate it when people called me Gabriel by mistake. Now I'm not sure why it bugged me._

I read the list at least ten times while my thoughts whirled and my heart raced. It wasn't signed, but it was obviously from Eric. He might have worked his brother's name into the last one just in case I had any doubts.

But then why not just sign it? Was he trying to give me a hard time about saying secret admirer notes were bad? This wasn't a note at all. It was a list. It was a list of mostly frivolous facts, but it was more than that. It was written partly to make me laugh and partly to help me get to know Eric better. Both of those goals meant Eric was on his way to becoming a bigger problem.

I fanned my face with the paper. I was still wearing my coat, and the fast pumping blood was making me overly warm. Snowflake was also meowing in circles around my ankles. I folded up the list, put it back in the envelope and dropped it into the recycling bin.

After I fed my cat and myself, I took the envelope out of the bin, which I knew I'd do before I even dropped it. Then I tucked it safely in the bottom of a drawer.

****

Going to work was now a bit stressful because I didn't know when I might see Eric or how I might react. Was I supposed to comment on either of the items he'd mailed to me? Was I supposed to ask how he got my address? I thought I knew the answer to that.

There had been a couple of Fridays when I noticed his car ahead of me as we left the church parking lot. He drove straight past the street where I turned off. My house was the second one from the corner so it would have been easy for him to see where I ended my trip if he happened to be behind me. But I couldn't point that out without admitting I'd been keeping track of his car. He could not know how vulnerable I was to... well, to him.

He'd only ever been in the library between four and six so I was able to concentrate on work in the morning and early afternoon. When I didn't see him at all for a few days, I began to relax. Maybe he regretted the impulses that landed in my mailbox. And maybe he was only waiting to catch me off guard.

I was scanning a shelf for a misfire when he appeared at the end of it and said, "Hello." Then he apologized for startling me.

I didn't believe he was sorry because he looked highly amused by my reaction. "I think you scared me on purpose."

"Why would I do that?" he asked, which was not a denial.

I had no answer because I wanted to laugh, and I wanted to run away. Eric was near me so suddenly I was overwhelmed by him being near me. I was trying to get my brain to exert control over the situation.

"Mrs. Bentley sent me to ask if you want help checking the top shelf," Eric said. "She trusts my ability to count."

I felt a self-conscious smile. "She hasn't seen you intentionally putting books in the wrong places."

"Do you want me to do the top shelf?"

"I have a stepstool." I gestured to the black step beside me. The top shelf wasn't so high I couldn't see it, but standing higher was more comfortable than tipping my neck back. "And it's easier if I go in order."

"Okay. I guess I'll... I'll get something to put away." He backed up slowly.

I wasn't clueless. I knew when he asked if I wanted his help he was really asking if I wanted him to work close enough to chat. I intended to casually send him away as though I was clueless. But when he looked disappointed, my stupid emotions took over. "It'd be more helpful for you to do a whole vertical section than to go across the top."

He perked up and waved a hand up and down the aisle. "Which way are you going?"

"I just started," I said. "You can work behind me and see if we meet up at the other end."

"Sounds like a challenge."

"I'll be going slowly to make sure I don't miss anything."

"Me, too," Eric said. "When you check twice as many shelves as I do, it's because I'm being extra careful."

"Right." I rolled my eyes at him because that seemed to be the reaction he was going for, then turned back to remember where I was when he got there.

We worked quietly, though I heard humming in my head as I read the numbers in time to a bouncy tune. For once, I didn't feel distracted by Eric's presence, I felt energized by it.

"Julia," he said after some time, "did you get anything you liked for Christmas?"

The humming stopped as abruptly as if someone had pulled the plug. Was that simple small talk or was he asking if I got his card? If he didn't ask directly, I didn't have to answer directly. I was wearing something that could keep it at small talk. "My mom gave me these earrings actually." I pulled my hair back to show the silver swirl on one ear.

"Those are pretty," he said.

"I guess they're technically from both my parents, but we all know my mom does the shopping."

He nodded. "Sounds like our family. Gabriel and I finally convinced her this year that we should stop doing gift exchanges now that we're adults. The trade-off was having to go shopping with her for some charity presents."

"How'd that go?"

"Torturous." He sighed dramatically. "She dragged us to three different stores for what seemed like a very simple list. But she looked happier than she has opening probably anything I've ever bought her."

"Quality time," I mumbled.

Eric cocked his head at me. I think he heard what I said but realized I was talking to myself and therefore had not expressed a complete thought.

"Sorry," I said. "I was thinking out loud. Are you familiar with the love languages?"

"That's a book, right? I've heard of it, but I haven't read it."

I nodded. "Yeah. I think the concept, that people feel loved in different ways, is really interesting. And I was just thinking maybe your mom likes quality time over gifts."

"Maybe." Eric looked thoughtful before he smiled. "Or maybe I'm just terrible at giving gifts."

I wished I knew if that was actually funny or if I was laughing at nothing again. I wiped the smile off my face and said, "I suppose I don't have enough information to rule that out."

Eric smiled at the jab. He was holding his finger on the shelf behind him to mark his place and turned back to it as an older woman turned into the aisle with us. She didn't appear to pay either of us any attention as she scanned the shelf. I returned my eyes to the books as well.

I was aware of the woman pulling a book from the shelf and moving away. I glanced back and saw that Eric was still focused on numbers. We enjoyed a few more minutes of companionable silence. Then I actually found a misfire. There were a lot fewer of them among the adult books so I was kind of happy to find one. I read the front of the book only because it was in front of me.

"What's wrong?" Eric asked.

"Nothing," I said.

"You just scoffed at that book. I mean, after you looked at it, not because it was in the wrong place."

"Oh, I..." Though I didn't realize it at the time, I may have snorted when I saw the book. "It might not be terrible," I said. "I just noticed the words 'follow your heart' in the subtitle, and I hate that phrase. It seemed appropriate."

"Hang on one minute." Eric looked at his finger marking his place and moved it over the last few books to finish a row, then put his arm down as he turned back to me. "What you said begs a lot of questions. Why do you hate that phrase? And why is it appropriate if you don't like it?"

"Follow your heart sounds like let your emotions lead you and do whatever you feel like, which is like saying we shouldn't bother having knowledge or self-control. It's advice to act like a two-year-old. It wasn't very nice, but I was thinking it was appropriate that someone looking at this book would not be able to reshelve it properly."

"You don't, um, think people should pay attention to what they want?"

"That's not what I mean," I said. "Likes and dislikes, people should be aware of those. But emotions are irrational. I prefer to follow my head."

Eric nodded hesitantly, as though he was listening but not necessarily agreeing with me. His eyes seemed to skim over the top of my head before they met mine. "What does your head say about me?" he asked.

"You have blue eyes."

Those eyes dropped to the floor for a moment and returned to me with a completely unreadable expression.

Of course, I didn't try to make out his thoughts very long because I was too busy being horrified by my own. You have blue eyes!? Here I was arguing that following my head was the smart thing to do and stating the most obvious fact was the best I could do. "They're very blue," I said. I meant to explain my momentary distraction, and it came out like a mawkish compliment and not an intelligent thought. "I mean, I couldn't help noticing the color and how yours are just like Gabriel's. I guessed you two were brothers before anyone told me."

"I've been told we look alike a few times." He didn't sound exasperated or anything but definitely not impressed by my insight.

"Well, that was my first thought," I said. "If you want anything deeper, you might have to be more specific."

He said, "Oh," and nodded as though what I'd said made sense.

It seemed I had successfully passed off my bungling as his fault. But it had been an unexpected question. Now that my brain was processing it, I could think of a lot of different ways to answer. Mostly though, I thought we could be really good friends if I could only figure out how to not be attracted to him. That might happen if he'd stop coming by to talk to me. But if we weren't talking, then we weren't friends. How was that for complex thought?

I had turned around to have these thoughts while I found the right place for the book that started the conversation.

"Okay, what do you think…" Eric trailed off as I faced him again. "Does your head tell you that you can start to talk about…. important things with someone you've known five months?"

I focused on the trivial part of the question to stay calm. "I think you need to check your math."

"Almost five months," he said. "It's called rounding. And I think what you're doing is called stalling."

I smiled what probably looked like a guilty smile. "Stalling isn't a no. You're making me nervous with this buildup to *important things*. Go ahead and ask."

"I've just been wondering… You said something a few weeks ago about your parents giving you a hard time about being a religious nut – your words – and," he paused to make sure it was clear he wasn't calling me that, "most people I know who consider themselves Christian got their faith from their parents so I'm curious about your story."

"Should I get out the sock puppets for this?" I asked.

He smiled knowingly.

I realized I'd inadvertently confirmed that I'd read his note. Time to move on. "Okay, I did… sort of… get my faith from my parents. I grew up kind of culturally Catholic. My parents sent me to religious ed classes just enough to get the Sacraments. We went to church – well, my mom and my brother and I – went something like once a month. I figured I would stop as soon as I got out of the house. I know my brother did. When I was in college though, I had a different roommate every year and one year I even had two and that's a whole other story. Anyway, the roommate I had my second year, she came from a similar background, and she wanted to go to church a couple of times just so she could tell her parents she did if they asked. She wanted me to go with her, and I thought why not?"

Eric nodded. He was with me so far.

"So we went one Sunday, and I found out that the priest there was really funny. Also, I'd recently had a falling out with my best friend so my weekends were suddenly wide open. I started going to church sometimes on Saturday *and* Sunday partly because I didn't have anything else to do. And... I started paying attention." My hands came up. Sometimes I talked with my hands when I got excited. "When my mom was dragging me to church, I was mentally checked out the whole time. When I was choosing to go, I was listening. I would hear something in one of the readings and be like, I remember hearing about this story when I was a kid. I'd go home and pull out a Bible to see what happened next. I was starting to figure out why we did things and not just what we were supposed to do. I was learning what people mean when they say they're on fire for Jesus."

"I can still see it," Eric said. He seemed amused by my waving hands.

The fire was still in me, but I'd learned some self-control. "Well, back then I was a little too... Let's just say I figured I only needed to explain a few things to my parents and they'd be as excited as I was. It didn't quite work out that way. When I say they give me a hard time, it's not entirely undeserved. Either I'm not cut out to be an evangelist, or my parents need a much more subtle, long-term approach. We've mostly accepted where the other is. They just sometimes make jokes like... Oh, we better pray before we eat or Julia will tell on us the next time she talks to God."

"That's good," Eric said. "I mean, not that they make jokes, but that they don't really bother you. I was afraid there was some strain there."

I shook my head. "You get along pretty well with your family, too, right? You were willing to go shopping with your mom."

"As a Christmas present," he clarified. "But, yeah. We don't have a weekly family meal like the Zieberts. It's more spontaneous." He shrugged. "And I usually sit with them at church. Family time doesn't always have to involve talking."

I nodded. I agreed.

"You know, you could sit with us, too, if you ever feel like company in the pew. Although..." He sort of looked like he wanted to rescind the offer as a thought snuck up on him. "Well, my mom might not be able to let that go without *some* talking."

His mom would likely read into our relationship something that was not in the relationship. I would not be sitting with Eric's family during church, but I nodded politely at the uncomfortable offer.

"What are you doing to celebrate New Year's?" he asked with a sudden switching of gears.

"I plan to celebrate by writing the wrong year on everything for half of January."

He laughed. "What a coincidence. Me, too."

I put my finger on the shelf behind me in a subtle indicator that I should get back to work. I needed to get back to work before the conversation shifted any more towards a joining of plans.

Eric noticed. "I'm taking too much of your time," he said. "I'll finish checking this shelf, then get out of your way."

That was exactly what he did. He worked quickly and got my attention just long enough to wave before he left. I felt sad and relieved when he went. Emotions weren't just stupid, they were inconsistent. I congratulated myself again for not letting them rule me.

8

I had to wait a week into January for the next young adult meeting at St. Jude's. Eric stopped in the library once more, but I was actually busy so we only talked for a minute.

Emily called me a couple of times. I enjoyed hearing about the grand opening of Joseph's Gym and her teaching debut. She counted it a success because the class was full, and she didn't fall down. I also confirmed when she'd be at Burger Brothers the following week. That was important because I'd decided to make a move. I figured the best way to stop fretting about Eric, to maybe stop thinking about him, was to start thinking about someone else.

So far, it was working. At least, I was doing a good job of convincing myself it was working. I was thinking more about my plan than about Sean specifically. He usually left the meetings quickly, and I didn't want to chase him out of the room. I thought I'd have a better chance catching him before we started.

That's why I was early. I was sitting in my car to keep warm. I hadn't parked very near the door so I was definitely going to be cold by the time I got inside. But I didn't want anyone to notice me sitting in my car. Ruth and Gabriel were the first to arrive. Ella was with them, and I saw Isaac and Jessica pulling into the lot as they got the door unlocked. I shut off my heater and followed the forming group.

I'd never been there early enough to help set up, but I'd seen the result enough to know how. We got the tables folded up and the chairs pushed into a circle. Grace was awake so Jessica took her out of the carrier to hold her. I admired the baby as an excuse to stay standing while the others claimed seats. Then I chose a chair with empties on either side. I hoped Sean would happen to sit close enough to make this easy on me. Or quick anyway.

Heather walked in and made a beeline for the seat on my right. "Hi, Julia," she said. She looked happy to see me.

I tried not to look *un*happy to see her. It wasn't her personally, I just didn't want an audience. The fuller the room got, the more likely I'd chicken out on my plan.

"Well, my holidays were awful," Heather said. "This was the first Christmas since my parents split. I spent the morning at my mom's house trying to pretend I wasn't going to see my dad later. Then I spent the afternoon with my dad, who grilled me for details on my mom the whole time. I think he wants them to get back together – which of course I would like – but I don't want to be part of it. And I got no sympathy from either of my brothers. They were like, 'Stop whining. It is what it is.'"

"I'm sorry," I said. "That does sound like a less than pleasant Christmas."

She huffed, then leaned closer to whisper, "And I bumped into Adam at Seymour's yesterday. He completely ignored me, but I couldn't tell if he didn't want to talk to me because he associates me with Kayla or if she told him something about me or if maybe he really didn't see me because I was kind of trying to hide."

I nodded. I also noticed Sean had just entered the room. He sat on the opposite side of the circle and didn't immediately engage with anyone else. "I'll be right back," I said to Heather.

I crossed the room taking slow, deliberate breaths. There was no need to be nervous. It would be embarrassing if he turned me down, but it would not hurt my feelings. I was not asking him out anyway, I'd rehearsed my words to try to make that clear. The first step was simply to find out if we had any common goals. "Hi, Sean," I said as I sat down.

"Hi."

"I want to ask if you'd be willing to meet me for dinner sometime so we can try to get to know each other," I said. "Just something friendly but away from the rest of the group."

Sean's eyes bugged out behind those awful glasses. Seconds ticked by, I think. I can't be sure because it didn't seem as though time was moving at all. "Uh…" He just stared at me until finally he said, "When?"

"I have to work tomorrow," I said. I didn't work late enough that I couldn't have dinner with someone. I thought I'd have more energy on a day off though. I did not have to work on Sunday, but neither did Emily. She was my support system, just in case. "How about Wednesday?"

Sean pulled out his phone and tapped at the screen without saying anything. I assumed he was either checking his calendar or trying to pretend I hadn't asked a question. I glanced around the room while I waited to find out which. I returned a smile from Sebastian, who was in the process of claiming the seat I had vacated.

Heather jumped up and scurried to sit next to my new seat. I thought it likely had as much to do with wanting to be near me as not wanting to be near Sebastian. He put his head down and rubbed a hand over his forehead. The guy could tell Heather's movement had at least something to do with him.

Her movement also trapped me. We'd played more musical chairs than adults of any age should be playing so I couldn't move again. That might have been for the best. If Sean did not want to meet me later, remaining next to him anyway could prove it wasn't a big deal. And if he did agree, I could hardly act as though dinner was fine but sitting next to him was not.

"Why did you leave me over there?" Heather hissed in my ear.

"I just wanted to ask Sean something."

"What?"

"Nothing important."

Heather looked offended that I didn't want to tell her.

"I mean, I'll tell you later," I said.

She relaxed and nodded as though we were already sharing a secret.

I turned back to Sean to try to end my suspense.

His expression was uncertain. "Wednesday?"

"Yes," I said. "6 o'clock?"

He nodded slowly.

"Do you like Burger Brothers?"

He nodded again.

"Great." I smiled encouragingly because I suddenly felt as though I was trying to convince him it was a good idea. My ego winced. "I'll see you there?"

He nodded, then immediately turned his eyes back to his phone.

I told myself it was a calendar thing as I felt a tug on my other arm. When I turned back to Heather, her eyes were wide.

She whispered, "Did you just ask him out?"

I shook my head. "It's not a date."

She looked speechless, for which I was grateful.

Eric came into the room. The distraction was actually welcome. He waved around the room before taking a seat.

"Just in time," Gabriel said. He flipped open a notebook. "We're going to talk about St. Therese of Lisieux today, but first a prayer. I thought we'd start with the Our Father for a change."

I laughed along with everyone else. Gabriel always started the meeting by leading us in The Lord's Prayer. And he always made a comment about it being a novel idea. I think we laughed because it felt good to be in a room full of people who shared the joke, even if it wasn't a funny joke. Though maybe it was a little funny.

"St. Therese is mostly known, by people who know anything about her, for her Little Way," Ruth said. "She wrote about this and the gist of it is that even the most mundane tasks serve God if they're done with love. We want to talk about... um... What are some things you do that could maybe be a little more joyful if you remember that you're serving God?"

Jessica raised her hand as she said, "Changing diapers. It's not even that awful. It's just that I feel like I do it a hundred times a day. I try to remind myself that it's one way that I'm loving my child, who is also God's child."

"You could have Isaac change a few," Heather said.

"He does." Jessica was quick to defend her husband.

Isaac shrugged sheepishly. "A few is probably accurate."

"Sometimes I deal with some difficult clients at work," Sebastian said. "I'm not sure I think of them as, uh, made in God's image."

"Sometimes they're probably not doing a great job of reflecting it," Isaac said.

There was a break that seemed like a good place for me to share. "I could use some help with cleaning," I said. "I mean, the last few years since I've been living on my own, I've realized how much my mom used to do for our family. Because of how messy things get. I have trouble feeling like it's worth it to keep the place clean when I don't yet have a family to keep it clean for. Does that make sense?"

"Sure," Eric said. "But taking care of yourself is important, too."

"Yeah, but…" It wasn't that I didn't take care of myself. I must not have expressed my thoughts well. "I believe the little way is about making small sacrifices for others. So it feels… I'm not really loving others when I make my bed since no one else will see it."

"I think I know what you mean," Ruth said. "I just have a tiny little apartment, and I can't say I feel as though I'm honoring God by cleaning the weird orange stuff out of my shower. But I look forward to having a family not so much to appreciate my effort but to have someone to take turns with."

"Hey, help would be nice, too," I said with a small laugh.

Jessica smiled. "Both are nice."

"Yeah, I, um…" Sebastian shifted in his chair, the one with the only empty seats in the room on either side of it. "As my mom has gotten older, she's had to let me take over some of the chores. It's been kind of hard for her. I had to put a lock on the door to the basement to get her to stop trying to navigate those steps with a laundry basket. And… well, I think it's helped me see that it is a blessing to be able to do those mundane tasks."

There was a moment of silence as we let the fairly profound thought sink in. I didn't know if Heather was the only person who had intentionally avoided Sebastian, but I still felt it was brave of him to speak from the apparently outcast position. Though it was sad to think he might be able to do it because he'd grown accustomed to it. I might have to confirm Emily's suspicions if Sean wasn't a good fit. But I'd also need to look into Heather's accusations. The man was a puzzle.

"I think we've talked before about how purpose helps," Gabriel observed. "Cleaning a bathroom just to make it clean is going to be less satisfying than cleaning it for someone you love or to utilize a gift from God."

"Purpose. That's my favorite word," Emily said. "I'm just in time."

Joseph walked in right behind her, and they filled in two of the seats by Sebastian.

There were a few greetings to acknowledge the new arrivals. I remembered that Emily had spoken of purpose before, both at our Friday night meetings and when we were at her house. It was the difference between making your life a vocation and simply drifting through it. It gave me some validation for my less than romantic dating plan. There was nothing wrong with using my head to purposely build a relationship on a logical foundation.

Isaac was explaining to Emily and Joseph what we'd been discussing when Emily's favorite word came up.

Joseph turned to me. "It's practice, too," he said.

"Practice for when, or if, I do have a family?"

He nodded. "There's that cliché that to have good friends you need to be a good friend. I think we can say something similar about spouses. Anything you do to prepare yourself – learning to clean up after yourself, sticking to a budget and so on – can be seen as a gift to your future spouse even if you don't yet know who that person will be."

"You know, people say that it's important to know what you want from a marriage," Jessica said. "I suppose it's just as important to know what you're bringing."

I thought that made sense. One of the guys I met online rejected me – well, said we weren't a good fit – because I wasn't adventurous enough. I'd let that hurt my feelings, but I was not an adventurous person. I should not have let a fact upset me. Everything we were saying went along with my attitude that a good marriage was more about choices than feelings. Although, if I'd been paying closer attention, I might have wondered why I was suddenly trying so hard to justify me to myself.

"Okay, so another thing about St. Therese is that she is said to have had visions from God." Gabriel glanced around the room to see if people were ready for him to move on. Seeing no objections, he continued. "Without talking about those visions specifically, we thought we could treat it as a what if. *If* God sent you a vision of the future, what would be something you might like to see or not see?"

"Nothing bad," Heather said right away.

"I don't know," Joseph said. "Wouldn't some advance notice be good? You could prepare yourself."

Heather shook her head. "I'd just be upset about it earlier. That's not helpful."

"What if it was something you were meant to prevent?" Sebastian asked.

"Well..." Heather scrunched up her face doubtfully. "The vision would have to include some very specific instructions."

Ruth turned to Ella. "What were you going to say?"

"Nothing."

"Come on. When he read the question, it looked like you had a thought."

"I..." Ella began to turn red. She spoke fast. "We'd just been talking about future spouses, and I thought if I knew who I'd end up with then I would not have to date anyone else in the meantime." She waved a hand to indicate someone else could talk now.

"Oh, I like that idea," I said. "If God could just point someone out, I wouldn't have to spend time figuring it out for myself."

"But," Heather said, "the guy would have to get the same vision. Otherwise, I'd have to convince... It'd just be a lot better if we started on the same page."

Emily was laughing. "I can just imagine going up to some guy like, 'Hey, God told me we're getting married so…' He'd run screaming."

"Exactly," Heather said.

I found her description amusing, as did a few others. Joseph gave her a playfully disapproving look. "You imagine approaching some guy?"

"I mean, before…" She smiled. "Would that have worked on you?"

He answered slowly. "I might have been willing to explore the possibility that you were a very faith-filled woman and not just nuts."

Emily shook her head like she didn't believe him.

"He would have," Heather said, rolling her eyes at Joseph, "only because you're very pretty."

"Not *only*," Joseph said. Then he quickly moved on. "Getting back to the original question, I wouldn't mind some regular everyday visions. I've generally had a sense of peace about major decisions, like opening the gym. But all the little things I pray about… It'd be nice to get some clear guidance like… Yes, you should call that guy one more time. No, that's not too much for an advertising budget. No, that's not too many kids at once."

"I don't know," Ruth said. "I mean, that would be nice, but wouldn't too much guidance sort of take away some free will?"

"No." Sebastian jumped in. "God has given us a lot of guidance right there in the Bible, and people manage to ignore it all the time."

"True," Isaac said. "But you gotta admit there'd be a difference between… Let's say you're tempted to tell a little white lie and on the one hand you have a whisper from your conscience that can be easily shoved aside and on the other you have God in all his glory showing you the exact negative consequences of that lie."

I squirmed at the mention of ignoring my conscience. I doubt I was the only one though. We'd all been there.

Ruth moved us along with some fun facts about St. Therese, few of which were actually fun. The poor woman lived in a convent governed by her sister and died when she was only twenty-four. We finished with the planned questions early but found plenty to chat about until 9:30.

I thought I should say something to Sean as we left about seeing him soon. He was the first one out of the room, with no backward glance. Emily and Joseph were right behind him, holding hands and looking cute.

I was honestly happy for them. Emily had thrown herself into the relationship so quickly that I worried she might be too attached to see any potential problems. But I still hoped everything would work out for them. That's where my mind was when Eric snuck up on me. Not on purpose of course. I'd been watching people leave and noticing that Gabriel and Sebastian were unfolding tables like they knew what they were doing when I realized Eric was right in front of me.

"Hey, Julia," he said. "You and Snowflake getting along better?"

"Of course." I pushed up the sleeve of my sweater to show him the scratch was nearly healed. "She's a nice kitty." I'd already explained that we'd been playing when she scratched me. It was an accident.

"Glad to hear it." He glanced at Heather, who was glued to my elbow, before he said, "I guess I'll see you soon." Then he left.

Heather waited until we were alone in the hallway before she lifted her eyebrows expectantly. "So you're going out with Sean?"

"Not really," I said. "I just thought we'd try to talk over dinner. I would like to get married someday, and I don't think God is going to tell me who to pick so I might as well check out the options."

"Yeah, but... Eric seems interested in you, and he is way cuter."

"Weren't you just giving Joseph a hard time for wanting to date Emily because of her looks?"

"I wasn't giving anyone a hard time," Heather said. "I was just being realistic." She shrugged. "I mean, I know why I'm still single."

"That's a terrible thing to say," I said. But at the same time, I didn't know what to say to refute it. Heather wasn't the sort of woman people looked at and thought, *Wow, she's beautiful.* I knew she wouldn't believe me if I said it. She was a little pudgy, though well proportioned and nowhere close to ugly. There was no reason to think she wasn't attractive to some guys, and she only needed one. How did I say that without highlighting that others might not be interested? I settled for the lamest answer. "You just haven't met the right guy." But then I thought of something else. "And wait a minute! You're the same age as me so I think you just insulted me, too."

She smiled at that. "I guess that means pretty people can be single longer." The smile faded. "Kayla used to... She's a lot prettier than I am."

"Did she say that?" I was torn between outrage at this supposed friend and frustration that Heather had taken it to heart.

"No. Not exactly." Heather paused. We'd stopped walking in front of the door so we could finish the chat before stepping into the cold. "Kayla was the only one in our group in a serious relationship. She used to offer joking advice to the rest of us – particularly me since I'd definitely gone the longest without – joking advice about clothes that weren't flattering and that maybe a nose job wasn't so drastic for some people." Heather put her hand on the door. "I never realized how mean her jokes were."

"If it didn't sound like sour grapes," I said, "I could point out that Kayla is now as single as you are."

Heather looked as though she was about to laugh, then said, "That does sound like sour grapes."

"Maybe. And maybe it just proves that good looks can help, but real love doesn't depend on it." And as far as I was concerned, physical attraction just got in the way.

9

I think I actually liked Mondays. Lillian did a cool storytime. I laughed as much as the kids, and I couldn't even see what she was doing. I was only listening from the next room. Sami came in to earn another hour of community service. She told me how her grandmother had been walking at Joseph's Gym in the mornings and was so excited to show off Sami's art – a painting of Lake Erie in winter – to all her friends. She sounded proud. And I think she even left without forgetting anything.

Two high school boys came in to put away books as well. They always came in together and usually did more talking than working. I wasn't in a position to criticize, and they were still helpful. They also made me laugh because they kept coming up to the desk to apologize for being slow, which contributed to them being slow.

All in all, it was a good day. Snowflake zoomed onto the porch when I got home. It was a nice way to be welcomed. I knew that at least part, and possibly most, of her excitement came from the fact that I was about to feed her. Nevertheless, it felt wonderful to have a living creature happy to see me. I pulled off one of my gloves to run my hand along her back before I grabbed the mail and opened the door.

I tossed the mail onto my kitchen table before I went about getting comfortable. I was being ridiculous. I'd caught sight of a white envelope. I hadn't even checked for a return address. I had deliberately not checked for a return address because I wanted to hope it was another letter from Eric, which was absolutely the last thing I should hope for.

I popped some leftovers into the microwave while I opened a can for Snowflake. I was doing a terrible job of pretending I didn't care what had come in the mail. It probably wasn't anything interesting anyway. I didn't know why I was letting myself get worked up for disappointment.

I sat at the table with my dinner and slowly, casually, moved aside what was partially covering the mysterious envelope. I was shocked to see my name and address in handwriting I recognized. All of my stalling had been to allow hope for something I didn't actually believe. And yet, there it was.

I gently loosened the flap, still trying to fool myself into thinking it didn't matter, and pulled out a sheet of paper. It was another list.

1 - My handwriting is terrible.
2 - Sometimes I state the obvious.
3 - I still like lists. (see above)
4 - I'm a careful driver. Now.
5 - I can draw a stick person.
6 - I'm not really a cat person, but I don't mind them.
7 - I like pizza. This is not obvious. I once met someone who didn't.
8 - I think I want kids, but the idea of raising someone who might not choose heaven is terrifying.
9 - I still haven't found the library book I lost three years ago.
10 - The kids in Joseph's class thought it was hilarious every time he threw me.

There was still no name. I mean, my name was on the envelope, but the list had no signature. That bugged me. I knew it was from Eric. He knew I knew it was from him. So why not sign it? Did he think leaving it ostensibly anonymous turned it into something romantic?

He was not allowed to do that. We were friends. Sending secret admirer notes that weren't secret was crossing a line. If that's what he was doing. Maybe he was trying to be funny. I'd told him secret love notes were stupid. He probably didn't think I'd find them romantic. Not that I did.

I pushed aside any subtext and reread the content. Most of it did make me laugh. A few numbers were more serious. The most worrisome were the ones that seemed to beg for follow-up questions. Joseph was throwing him around and the kids thought that was funny? I wanted to hear about that. Something happened that turned him into a careful driver? That was a story, too. I read the list a few more times while I ate and then tucked it into the bottom of a drawer with the first one and the only Christmas card that hadn't yet landed in the recycling bin.

****

Snowflake liked to play a hunting game. She would hide under the couch while I rolled a small jingling ball around the room. Eventually, she would spring and pounce on the ball. It almost always startled me. I wish I knew if she did that on purpose or if she was only focused on the ball.

I reluctantly stopped the game when I needed to get ready to meet Sean at Burger Brothers. I stood in front of my closet for a long time thinking about what to wear. It wasn't a date. I didn't want to be too casual though. I should still want to make a good impression out of respect for him as a person who had agreed to give me some of his time. I was wearing jeans and a t-shirt for hanging out with my cat. I grabbed a blue fair isle sweater. It was pretty and warm and I could imagine it looked as though I was dressing up without dressing up.

Snowflake was stretched out on my bed grooming herself as though she also needed to make a good impression. I smiled at the thought and continued into the bathroom to check my reflection. The sweater was fine, nice even. My hair looked fine. A few strands had escaped the low pigtails, but it sort of looked like I did that on purpose.

My eyes were the only problem I saw. There was no enthusiasm. I wasn't nervous. In fact, brutal honesty told me the only emotion I was feeling was some serious reluctance. I wanted to stay home with a cat purring against the side of my leg while I read a book.

I stared into those light brown, reluctant eyes and gave myself a mental pep talk. This was yet another example of why following your heart was a bad idea. My long-term goal was a husband and children, and I wasn't going to find those sitting on the couch with Snowflake. Time to overcome my weak emotions and be willing to follow through on my very logical plan for the evening. If I wanted a husband, I needed to spend time with guys who might be looking for a wife.

Now I looked fiercely determined, which was probably still not the most flattering expression to wear to this meeting. Appointment? It wasn't a date, but every other label I slapped on it sounded… It was time to go to whatever it was. I said goodbye to Snowflake and imagined that she wished me luck.

It was a little before six so I wasn't surprised that Sean wasn't there yet. There was a line at the register. I walked up to the pickup window and waved at Emily in the kitchen. She looked busy. I debated about getting in the line to save a place for Sean.

A vaguely familiar woman on roller skates came to a quick stop at my elbow. "Hi, honey," she said. "You look lost. Can I help you?"

Reluctant, determined, lost. My progression did not bode well for the evening. "I'm meeting someone here," I said. "I don't want to get in line if it'll be my turn to order before he gets here."

"Hmm. I don't think I can help with a timing problem." The woman gave a friendly smile. "You're welcome to have a seat while you wait if that's what you decide."

I nodded and thanked her before she rolled away, spinning as she did so. The spin was not especially graceful, but she didn't hit anyone. When I scanned the restaurant again, I saw Sean coming through the door.

I walked up to him trying to think about how close my expression came to looking happy to see him. I was at least happy not to be waiting anymore. "Hi, Sean. Thanks for coming."

He nodded at me and mumbled, "Hello."

I motioned towards the line, and we moved that way together. "What are you going to get?" I asked.

"Cheeseburger," he said.

That sounded good. I was thinking the same thing. It was a burger place though. I didn't think there were a lot of choices. We didn't talk as we waited our turn. The man at the register was the same mustached man who grouchily made Emily the special shakes. He was scarier without Emily doing the talking. I planned to not mess around.

Sean nodded for me to order first. I asked for a cheeseburger and paid for it myself. I thought proper etiquette said I should pay for both of us since I issued the invitation. But Sean wanted to pay for his own, and I hoped that might solidify that we were not on a date. Not yet. If things went well, if we found a lot of common ground, we'd make some decisions about status and stuff.

The man at the register showed a spark of recognition as Sean opened his mouth to order but not in a good way. I was afraid things were about to get complicated

Sean said, "Two cheeseburgers, please. I don't want ketchup on either of them. Put pickles only on one. The one with the pickles should have a toasted bun. Go a bit heavy on the mustard, and you're still overcooking the burgers. Just cut a minute off the grill time."

In the months we'd been attending young adult meetings together, I had never heard Sean string so many words together. He picked a lousy time to voice opinions as I heard a huge sigh as his order was entered. Sean either didn't notice the annoyance or didn't care that he caused it.

We took a seat while we waited for the order. Silence settled over our table. It wasn't a comfortable, friendly silence. It was the silence of two bored people who had nothing to say to each other. I decided to plunge in and not waste the opportunity.

"Okay, Sean," I said, "how about we just do this like an interview?"

"Do what?" he asked.

"Find out if we have, well, things to talk about."

He made a gesture that seemed to indicate I had permission to proceed.

"Even if it seems to be jumping ahead, I think the most rational place to start is… to… I'll just ask. Are you *eventually* looking to marry *someone?*"

He nodded, and perhaps more importantly, didn't appear shocked at the question. Maybe we *could* do this like an interview. "What about kids?" I asked.

"Three," he said.

"Three as in exactly three kids?" While I was glad to hear he'd given the matter some thought, something about the definitive answer didn't sit right with me. Children weren't like choosing a meal where you simply decided how hungry you were at a particular point in time. I thought it should be more of an ongoing conversation.

He nodded again. "Yeah. Two seems kind of stereotypical and one would end up spoiled."

"Why would one end up spoiled and not two?" I asked, trying to sound more interested than I was.

He just squinted at me as though he didn't know why I was asking.

"Doesn't whether or not a child is spoiled depend more on discipline than the number?"

He shook his head. "I mean, spoiled by attention, not stuff. But you sort of have a point. I'd be sure to let my wife know if she was doing something wrong with the kids."

I couldn't help thinking of my brother and his wife, that someone needed to tell them what they were doing wrong. I didn't like that it sounded like a judgmental thought, but I liked even less how unhappy his whole family seemed all the time. What I liked least though, was Sean – a person who didn't have kids – sounding arrogant about having all the answers. Then it hit me that I didn't actually *know* he didn't have kids.

I should have started with more basic information. "You don't already have kids, do you? Or an ex-wife or any other…" *Don't say baggage, don't say baggage.* Sara and Brian's parents were divorced, and she once overheard her mom describe them as baggage when talking about a potential date. She was deeply hurt. Children should not be made to feel responsible for keeping their parents happy when the opposite was true.

Sean shook his head before I thought of a better way to finish my sentence.

"How old are you?" I asked.

"Thirty-two."

I tried to freeze my eyebrows. Thirty-two wasn't too old, but it was five years or so older than I would have guessed. "Have you lived in Andauk your whole life?"

He shook his head.

I waited until I realized he didn't intend to elaborate. "What do you do for a living?"

He shrugged.

I narrowed my eyes at him. What kind of answer was what? "You don't know?"

"I'm between jobs right now."

"Oh. I'm sorry."

He shrugged again.

I couldn't tell if he didn't consider it a big deal or just didn't want to talk about it. "Do you think of yourself as a careful driver?"

Now it was his turn to narrow his eyes at me. "What does that have to do with anything?"

Then I guess it was my turn to shrug. I'd just thought that two people trying to make a life together would end up going places together, and that would involve driving and... I waved away the question. "Do you like cats?"

"They're okay," he said, with zero enthusiasm. "But I have three dogs who probably wouldn't get along with one."

Poor Snowflake. That was something that could be worked around if we had the motivation though. I was trying not to doubt that motivation already. Such a quick dismissal would not be a reasoned, thoughtful response. As I tried to think of logical questions pertaining to whether or not we might work together, I found myself hoping he would answer whatever I came up with "incorrectly." That was hardly keeping an open mind.

Sean's mouth was open. I could see pieces of the second burger he was already inhaling. I realized I was relieved that we might not have much longer to talk. Relief was emotional. Where was my objectivity? Where was my plan to get what I wanted by simply evaluating the choices? I pushed aside any weak feelings to focus on some questions I'd thought about ahead of time. We didn't get through many before he crumpled up his wrapper and glanced at the door.

"You ready to go?" I asked.

He nodded and began to slide out of the booth without asking if I was also ready.

My question might have implied I was done. I stuffed my last bite into my mouth and moved to follow. Sean tossed his trash and mumbled a thanks as he passed me on his way to the door.

I was moving slowly on purpose because I hoped to stay and chat with Emily.

She apparently had the same idea. The doors to the kitchen swung open, and she came out carrying a rag and a spray bottle. She nodded me towards the table I'd just vacated. "So?" she asked as she began to spray it down.

I shook my head.

"Ruling him out already?"

"Let's just say he's moved to the bottom of the list for now," I said. He had said he generally preferred staying in to going out, and I didn't necessarily *not* want three kids. I wasn't sure I had enough objective cause to eliminate him. I had a feeling, however, that I wasn't on *his* list so mine might not matter.

"That's too bad," Emily said. She cast a furtive look towards the kitchen as she bent forward to wipe the seats. "Want me to introduce you to Luke while you're here?"

Moving down my very short list did not sound like a bad idea. "Okay," I said. "If you can do it without… um…" I wasn't sure how to put my thought into words. I was fine with being direct and somewhat obvious about my interest as long as it wasn't weird. This wasn't the wishy-washy, emotional, easily manipulated kind of interest.

Emily smiled. "Don't worry. I'll be subtle." She led me to the pickup window. Through it I could see Luke standing next to a teenage boy. They appeared to be chopping vegetables, but I didn't have a clear view of the work surface.

"Hey, Luke!" Emily called, waving him over.

Subtlety, thy name is not Emily Mayor.

He rolled his eyes as he peeled off his gloves. We already had common ground.

Emily continued as he approached the other side of the window. "Julia just had a lousy date. Do you want a chance to redeem your gender?"

Luke fixed me with a look so intense I took a step backwards. "When she says bad, she means boring, right? We're not talking about any kind of mistreatment?"

I shook my head at the overbearing concern, which ironically felt more threatening than anything Sean had said. "Do you know Sean?" I asked, pausing to realize I couldn't supply a last name if he asked for one. I clearly needed to practice pumping guys for information, yet I still hoped I would not do it enough to become good at it.

"Not well," Luke said. "We went to school together but haven't crossed paths much since."

I nodded.

"Sorry, guys," Emily said. "Chip's calling me." She rushed around me to head into the kitchen.

I hadn't heard anything so I assumed it was an excuse to leave me alone with Luke. But I glanced over Luke's shoulder and saw Emily's boss staring her down. That could have been interpreted as a summons.

"How long have you worked here?" I asked.

"Since high school." His expression darkened as he spoke, as though he was daring me to find something wrong with that answer.

I tried to smile pleasantly. Stability was on my list of desired qualities. "Your dad is one of the brothers on the sign?"

He only grunted, but I interpreted it as an affirmative response.

And just like that I was out of things to say. My brain was running through the list of questions to ask potential husband candidates, none of which I could ask Luke in this spur-of-the-moment meeting. Maybe I should go ahead and ask him out. Then we could get to an appropriate setting to start finding out what was important.

I could at least ask his last name. I was about to introduce myself properly to encourage him to do the same when he sighed heavily. Fortunately, he was looking over my shoulder so I knew it wasn't aimed at me.

I turned and saw the same old man I'd seen in the little gift shop, Jojo. He came in rubbing his hands together. He still wasn't wearing a coat, but based on the assortment of collars he had on at least half a dozen layers. The top one, a red and black flannel, was buttoned crookedly.

Luke and I watched as he stepped up to the register. I didn't mean to stare. The man walked with his arms outstretched like an airplane. It almost forced my attention. Chip met him on the other side of the counter. He didn't say hello or anything, just greeted him with an expectant expression.

Jojo put his arms down. He noticed Emily in the back and took a step away from the register to give himself room to dip into an elaborate bow, that she probably couldn't see past the counter. She waited for him to stand and then grabbed both sides of an imaginary skirt to curtsy in response. Jojo appeared delighted with what was apparently a regular exchange.

Chip shot Emily a stern glare like she was being a bad influence. Then he turned back to Jojo and said, "You wanna eat or what?"

The old man held out his palm and moved it in a circle.

"Fries today?"

Jojo's mouth dropped open in surprise.

Chip made no reaction to the shock. "Just the cheeseburger then?" he deadpanned.

Jojo closed his mouth slowly, then nodded slowly.

"One minute." Chip turned around. I noticed that he did not ask Jojo for any money.

"What made you go out with Sean anyway?"

Luke's sudden question brought me back to where my attention was supposed to be focused. And his tone suggested my reason was not crush-related. Perhaps that meant he would be open to a similar rational exploration of future goals. "Well... I'm just trying to find a guy who has things in common with me. Faith seems like a good place to start, and I met him at the young adult group. I saw you at St. Jude's at Christmas."

Luke ignored my hint completely. "You're not looking at Sebastian Jones next, are you?"

Because I *had* considered Sebastian, the accusation made me too defensive to correct him on where my sights currently sat. "Why?" I asked.

Luke shook his head with storm clouds in his eyes. "Don't be fooled," he said. "Just because he shows up at that church group doesn't make him a good guy. He was arrested again just a couple months ago."

I felt a gasp but tried to cover it. "For what?"

"Assault. Don't know why the charges never stick."

Was Heather right? Sebastian seemed so nice I hoped any violence was buried deep in his past. But a couple of months didn't leave much time for rehabilitation.

I stepped aside with my thoughts as Jojo moved to the pickup window to collect his burger.

Chip handed it over wrapped in white paper with a pair of knit gloves on top. "Put those on *after* you eat," he commanded.

The old man's hands closed around the small stack, but he dropped one of the gloves.

I bent to pick it up and hand it to him.

He gave me a very quick bow as he took it. Then he moved towards the exit at a pace that nearly qualified as a jog.

Luke was shaking his head when I looked back. "Third pair of gloves this month," he muttered.

I said nothing in response to what sounded like a serious lack of charity. I tried to summon enough charity of my own to admit I might not have the whole story.

"Good boy!" Emily's voice said before she appeared next to Luke on the kitchen side of the window.

I looked the direction she'd come from to figure out where the comment had been directed. "Were you just talking to the cash register?" I asked.

She nodded and gave a slightly embarrassed shrug.

Luke rolled his eyes. "All the time," he said.

"Well," Emily said, "perhaps if I had coworkers willing to carry on a conversation, I would not have to resort to talking to inanimate objects."

Her argument was strengthened as Luke simply sighed and walked away.

"I'm not the one who named the register," Emily said, loud enough for everyone in the kitchen to hear.

Chip glanced up – not at Emily, at the register – then looked back at whatever he was doing.

I thought Emily had a pretty good point about the lack of conversation.

"I guess I'll see you on Friday?" I said.

Emily nodded. "Call me tomorrow though for details on…" She gestured to the table where I'd been sitting with Sean.

10

Emily called me before I had a chance to call her. I filled her in on my brief dinner with Sean, but I did not tell her that I'd received another letter from Eric. This one made me laugh even more than the others. But it had also included his favorite prayer.

I hadn't told anyone about those letters. Not even Eric. Not exactly. A few items from his lists came up without me actually admitting how I... But not the latest list because I got that one after... Okay, Thursday was kind of eventful. I should start at the beginning.

Lillian cut it closer than ever. I was holding the books for storytime, giving myself a mental pep talk, when she rushed in the front door with a wave of cold morning air. I put the books down.

"Sorry I'm late," Lillian said as she peeled off her scarf and began to unbutton her coat. She said that every morning, but I saw more sincerity than usual in her eyes.

"I can hang up your coat," I said.

She smiled at the offer and handed me her coat and purse before she grabbed the books from where I'd left them. I heard kids' laughter by the time I returned from the back room. A couple of high voices sounded near hysterics. Lillian had evidently made one of her sillier entrances.

I went off in search of books that had been requested. My progress was slow because I kept taking less than direct paths to eavesdrop on storytime. I knew exactly when it was over. Lillian came up to me only a few minutes later. "I've been thinking," she said. "Your first storytime shouldn't be when I happen to be sick or something. I want you to do the one on Monday."

"Monday?" I felt my eyes widen. "As in this coming Monday?"

"You can do it," she said with an encouraging smile. "And now you have a few days to prepare."

I think she meant that I had a few days to panic. "Are you sure?"

"Definitely. It's past time for you to read to the kids." Lillian gave me an appraising look. "Way past time."

I did not agree about anything being past time, and I only agreed to lead the very next storytime because Lillian was my boss so I had to do what she said. Choosing the books was going to be difficult. Everything that came to mind did so because I'd heard Lillian read it recently. And obviously I couldn't read anything she'd just read.

I eventually had a nice stack of books picked out, more than I needed in fact. Extra books would allow me to eliminate any that gave me problems while I was practicing.

Somehow I missed Eric's entrance. It probably happened when I was trying to arrange a transfer on the phone while practicing character voices in my head. He was not there as a volunteer but as a patron. When I noticed Eric, he was already approaching the desk. "Hi," I said. I slammed the door on the heart flutters that tried to emerge at the sight of those familiar blue eyes. The flutters might have been amplified by having something to vibrate against.

"Hi, Julia," Eric said. He plunked two books in front of me and dangled his keys from the library card tab.

I took the keys to scan the card first, ignoring the way my fingers brushed his. I know. If I had really ignored it, it wouldn't be worth mentioning. I made my best effort to ignore it.

The top book was a fantasy. Most of the time, I tried to avoid noting which books people checked out because I felt nosy otherwise. I felt I was allowed and maybe even encouraged to be nosy with a friend. Especially when he tapped on the cover of the second book and said, "This will be our secret, right?"

It was nonfiction, a book on saints.

"When Gabriel or Ruth brings up some obscure saint and I have a fact to contribute and everyone is impressed with my knowledge, you'll just nod along like, yeah, Eric's really smart and not tell them you saw me with this. Okay?"

I smiled at the teasing tone. "You're getting this to impress someone?"

"Of course not," he said. "But if someone happened to be awed by my knowledge... I wouldn't mind."

"I'll play along," I said as I began flipping through the book's pages until I found an obscure-looking saint. "Because I'm sure if you read up on St. Spyridon, that'll just happen to be who we talk about this week."

"What if I have inside information?" Eric asked.

"Do you?"

"No." He dropped the joking attitude. "I actually thought I'd read more on some people we've already discussed."

Emily had been studying saints, too. If I had a more competitive nature, I might have felt compelled to up my own game. "Was Joseph throwing you again yesterday?" I said instead. This was where I revealed that I'd read his list without specifically saying I had.

Somehow, it felt less… intimate to talk about what was in the notes than the notes themselves. If we talked about the fact that he was sending me letters, we might have to talk about why.

Eric nodded as though my question didn't come from something not secret that I wanted to make secret. "He calls it an essay and the kids – and some of the adults – laugh."

"What?" I said. "Like trying?"

Now Eric looked confused.

"He *tries* to throw you?"

"No, he does," Eric said. "He's very good."

"But essay means try."

He squished his eyebrows together. "Not in this case, and by the way not when most people say it. Joseph means it the normal way, as in a paper."

"That makes even less sense," I said, pushing his books towards him.

He paused for a moment, then said, "This might be my fault," followed by a lopsided smile that made me want to agree that everything was his fault. The clammy hands, the way my stomach squeezed, the onslaught of distracting feelings I had to fight around him… that was all his fault. But that was obviously not what Eric was talking about.

"I should have started with a better explanation," he said. "Other than me and Master Bob, who's Joseph's instructor, everyone in the class is a beginner. Joseph was afraid they'd be disappointed to show up for a martial arts class and spend the whole time learning stances and how to line up and bow in and… so he started with a demonstration. He explained that they needed to first learn to form letters and words, then they'd be writing essays in no time. He's keeping up the analogy and throws me over his shoulder whenever he mentions an essay."

"Over his shoulder?" I said. I really didn't know what it meant to throw someone in hapkido, but I hadn't pictured anything that involved going over the shoulder of a man who was a bit over six feet tall.

"There are mats." Eric said this as though he was reminding me of something obvious.

I was still either impressed or horrified. "Can you...throw Joseph?"

"Not nearly as well." Eric shook his head. "I'm a much lower rank and very rusty. I have to kind of think my way through it whereas Joseph's just like boom, Eric is on the floor. That's what I think the kids find so amusing, that I'm always on the floor."

The guy was happily letting himself be tossed around to entertain and instruct kids. Darn it. I had to settle on impressed. I pushed the books even closer to his side of the counter to get him to leave before my defenses got any mushier.

Eric picked up the books, but he didn't take the hint to leave. He tapped on the saints book. "I assume you'll be at St. Jude's tomorrow night?"

I nodded. That was my plan.

"It starts at eight and you get off work at six?"

He said it like a question, but he knew both of those times were right. I felt a nervous tremble as I nodded again. There wasn't a good reason Eric would be confirming a window he already knew existed.

"I suppose you need to feed yourself in those two hours," he said.

"And Snowflake," I added. We could not forget about my cat. She was the reason I needed to go home after work. And if I needed to take two hours to put food in her bowl, I would do that.

"Right, the cat." Eric seemed to have forgotten about her. He also noticed someone getting into line behind him. "So Friday..." he said as he turned back to me. "I wondered if... but I... I'll see you at the meeting." He smiled hesitantly as he walked away.

Hesitantly, as though I hadn't been the one holding my breath. I didn't know if I should thank Snowflake or the cute old couple ready to check out some books. I gave them a genuinely large smile as they placed the stack on the desk.

When I got home an hour or so later, I smiled at Snowflake, too. I always smiled at Snowflake when she zipped onto the porch, and she was a cat so she probably thought I smiled only because I was so happy for the chance to serve her. She didn't have any idea I was thinking about something else, someone else.

My thoughts were really stuck on Eric though, especially when the only thing in my mailbox was a plain white envelope addressed in a familiar hand. I rushed into the house, dropped the books for storytime and my bag on the counter, and stuffed my gloves into my pockets. One of the gloves jumped back out. I left it on the floor while I tore open the letter still wearing my coat.

Somewhere in the back of my mind a feeling of unease was battling my excitement. I wasn't letting either of those emotions control me. Opening a letter was simply the logical thing to do upon receiving a letter. Reading the contents would give me the information inside.

The page was numbered, but I read it three times and still wasn't sure it was a list.

1 - I'm afraid I might not be a very good housekeeper. I can follow directions though. I could change habits that cause problems. Eventually.

2 – My favorite prayer is to St. Michael the Archangel. We had a book when I was a kid, fiction, that depicted him like some sort of superhero. He shielded kids from creepy-looking bad guys who tried to get them to make bad choices. Even more than the idea of warrior angels, I was fascinated by the idea of warrior angels who help keep temptations at bay. I guess that's why I like his prayer.

3 – I would never misfile a book on purpose.

4 – Yeah, I know I did. I'm trying to clarify that I only did that because you were watching. I wanted to see your reaction and intended to put it back.

5 – Okay. You did end up fixing that book. But only because you seemed to think it was funny. You did think it was funny, right? I saw you smiling.

6 – In my defense, I have reshelved quite a few books over the last few months. That must make up for making you move one.

7 – Really? How many more do you think I need to shelve? I could come in more often.

8 – You might have a point. I try not to distract you if you look busy, and I work much faster when you're not around so I can make up for it.

9 – No, I really do.

10 – I very rarely have imaginary conversations. I'm not sure I ever have before. Can I blame you?

I finally refolded the letter with a big smile on my face. It wasn't that funny. Most of it seemed written to make me laugh. He had correctly guessed most of what I would have said, too.

Snowflake was less amused. She was meowing in circles around my ankles, probably wondering if I had forgotten where I kept her food. I didn't care if my cat knew it took less than two hours to feed her so I filled her bowl. Then I rummaged through the kitchen to find something to feed myself.

I knew Emily got off work at eight. It was the reason she and Joseph were always late on Fridays. I spent the remaining time trying not to think about the latest letter, or Eric at all. Unfortunately, I'd inadvertently memorized most of it. That made it kind of hard to get out of my head.

I suppose it was good I had other things to worry about. Storytime mostly. Once I opened the books I'd brought home, I got absorbed in trying to adopt a silly persona. That was an awful idea. All my ideas were awful. My character voices all sounded the same. I was stumbling over simple words and losing my place on pages with three sentences. I was going to be a complete failure at storytime! How was that even possible? I'd known how to read for twenty years. It shouldn't be so hard to read a few picture books.

I was not having anything like a panic attack. That would have been one of the worst instances of emotions running amok. But my eyes had begun to water with the effort of holding back tears of frustration. When my phone rang, I remembered that I was planning to call Emily. I grabbed a tissue before I answered to make sure I didn't sniffle.

"Emily. Sorry I didn't call yet," I said. "I hadn't realized it was getting late."

"It's not that late," she said. "I had to call you as soon as I got home from work because… Guess what happened!"

Her excitement rang through the phone loud and clear. I didn't know if she really wanted me to guess or was only pausing for dramatic effect. "What happened?" I asked.

"Joseph asked me to marry him!"

"What? Really?"

"I know you think we're moving too fast."

"No, I..." I did, but I wasn't going to bring it up when she was so happy. "I just know you two have talked about marriage before so I was asking if this was a real proposal."

"Yes." Emily sighed sappily. "Tomorrow is his thirtieth birthday, and he said he wanted to start getting old knowing he had me to be old with or something like... Those weren't his exact words. He said it way more romantic."

I took her word for it. "Have you told your parents?"

"Not yet. I want... I don't know. They're going to be insanely happy and wanting to be involved, and I just want to enjoy it for myself for a couple of days."

"I think I actually know what you mean."

"We'll probably set a date sometime in the summer. Now tell me about you. Sean was a bust?"

"Yeah. It really wasn't terrible," I said. "Mostly I just got the impression that he wasn't interested at all."

"But I thought... I thought you didn't want anyone to be interested. It doesn't seem fair to date a guy who likes you if you don't like him." Emily didn't sound as though she was accusing me of being unfair, but rather as though she was trying to figure out what she was missing.

"That's not even close to what I meant," I said. "I don't want anyone to be emotionally invested in the beginning. We should be clear-headed. But I want someone who is interested in finding out what we have in common and helping me figure out if we could make a relationship work. But I felt like Sean was humoring me to get through the dinner as quickly as possible."

"Oh. I see," Emily said. "What did you think of Luke?"

"Uh…"

"Not great, I guess."

"Well, I barely talked to him," I said. "He seemed kind of bent out of shape about Chip giving gloves to that old guy. I don't know how harshly to judge him for that since the cost could add up if he's giving him gloves all the time, but if the guy really needs…"

Emily interrupted me with a disgusted noise and said, "Men are so unobservant."

"What do you mean?" I asked.

"It's the same gloves. There's a woman who – I think she's related to Jojo – she keeps returning the gloves. I don't know if she and Chip worked something out ahead of time or if she just found out he gave Jojo some gloves but… Anyway, she comes in and hands them to Chip without saying a word. He just tucks them under the counter to give Jojo the next time he comes in."

"Wow. How is Luke missing that?"

"He's, um, preoccupied with…" Emily hesitated. "Okay. I'm going to tell you something without going into details – Paula's been giving me too many details – but… Luke's kind of recovering from a divorce. His wife apparently blindsided him with the request and refused several attempts to work things out."

"Oh. Well, that's…" I processed that for a second. "That's too bad." I was honestly sympathetic but also beginning to think what the information meant for me. If he'd been burned, he might be more likely to embrace my idea of making a commitment based on rational reasons and nothing mushy. But probably not for a while.

"Yeah," Emily said. "It is. I only told you because… Well, if you decided to ask him out, you'd know it might not be you if he refused."

"Thanks. I don't suppose you want to help with my other problem." I absently opened one of the books in front of me while I spoke.

"What is it?"

"I have to do storytime on Monday."

"Storytime? That sounds fun," Emily said. "What's the problem?"

Emily sounded so confident and cheerful that I couldn't bring myself to tell her that I was afraid of storytime. I was afraid I'd freeze up, and Lillian would have to rush in and do it for me. "I'm just having trouble picking the books," I said.

"Oh. I bet there are a ton of good ones. But you'll figure it out." She seemed sure that I only wanted to vent and wasn't really asking for help.

I knew that was the impression I'd given. We talked only a bit longer, mostly about some ideas she had for her wedding. I didn't mind. Frankly, I was impressed she'd turned the conversation to me at all with such big news on her mind.

When I put the phone down, I opened one of the kids' books and stared at a picture of a bunny wearing sock puppets. I was mad at myself for feeling a bit envious of Emily. Talk about an unproductive emotion. But she was doing it wrong. She was chasing a guy who gave her warm fuzzies, and it was working. I was trying to do it the intelligent way and was only spinning my wheels.

I was even angrier at myself for wanting to call Eric though. I wanted to tell him the things I'd been afraid to tell Emily. I wanted to hear his advice about my storytime fears. I wanted to know he was listening. Fortunately, I had been smart enough to know what he'd been hinting at when he tried to exchange numbers.

11

Eric probably wasn't waiting for me. He was standing in the hallway when I arrived for the Friday night meeting. He was looking at something on his phone. I'm sure it was only a coincidence that he put it in his pocket the same time I reached him. "Hi, Julia," he said.

I greeted him without stopping because if he was finished with whatever he'd been checking then he was ready to enter the room with me. He did come in right behind me, and he took the chair to my right. I could not pretend that wasn't deliberate. But I could imagine it was only because we were friends.

Ruth and Gabriel, Ella and Sebastian were all there. They had gotten the room organized but were just standing around chatting. Every seat was empty when Eric claimed one next to me. I caught Ruth's eye and gave a quick wave, which she returned.

"Sorry I didn't stay to help on Thursday," Eric said. "I thought you seemed pretty busy."

I only smiled in response because there were too many things I could say. If I looked busy, wouldn't that be a good time to help? Unless I was too busy to help him help. I thought it best not to think about it.

"Would you have some work for me tomorrow?"

"There are always books at the library," I said. And on Saturdays, there were more people so I was busier. I definitely shouldn't comment on that. I wanted to tell him that I was going to do storytime, and I might have except that Heather came in right then and practically dove into the chair on my other side.

"Julia!" She kind of hissed my name and motioned for me to lean closer to her. She widened her eyes expectantly and said, "So?"

I didn't know what she expected. "What?" I asked.

Heather sighed and leaned a bit closer. "Your date with Sean. How was it?"

I'd pretty much forgotten it happened. She was whispering, but I glanced around the room anyway. It was filling up. I saw two new faces and no sign of Sean. I took a moment to hope that if he wasn't coming that it had nothing to do with me. Then I lowered my voice to address Heather. "It wasn't a date," I said, "and it was..." I just finished with a shrug. That seemed the best description.

She nodded with an expression that looked very much like I told you so. Her eyes looked over my shoulder, then meaningfully back at me.

I could tell she was suggesting something to do with Eric so I just shook my head.

Heather nodded, a tiny yet forceful nod.

I answered with a similarly small but adamant shake.

She was nodding again when I noticed Ruth watching us. I got the impression she knew what we were talking about, possibly even better than I did. My face began to grow warm at the childishness of our silent conversation. Heather and I needed a topic we could discuss out loud. "Has Emily told you her news?" I asked.

She seemed to forget all about Eric but stayed huddled close. "What news?"

Oops. I'd expected her to start gushing with wedding talk. "Oh. I... I should let her tell you herself."

"Come on," Heather said, "you can't tell me someone has news and then not tell me what it is. That's mean."

"I'm sure she'll get a chance to tell you tonight."

"What if I guess?" Heather said.

Fortunately, we were distracted before she came up with her first guess. Jessica came in carrying the cute baby. Isaac was right behind her carrying a bunch of baby stuff.

"It's one of the birthday boys!" Ruth exclaimed. "As soon as Joseph gets here, we're going to sing to both of you."

Isaac smiled, but he said, "I don't think that will be necessary."

"Yes, it is," Ruth said. "Number one, because thirty is a big deal, and we have to acknowledge it. And number two, because I need to set a precedent to make everyone sing to Ella next month."

Ella looked at the floor and turned slightly red in advance.

Isaac took a seat next to Jessica and accepted some birthday wishes from the two new women on his other side. They looked young. At twenty-six, that wasn't a thought I had about other adults very often. I wondered if they might barely qualify.

"Let's begin with the usual prayer," Gabriel said. "Just this once." He flipped open a notebook and smoothed his tie while everyone quieted and put their hands together. He made a brief yet reasonably eloquent plea for a productive meeting before he led us in an Our Father. Then he turned expectantly to Ruth.

"Okay," she said. "We picked St. Monica to talk about this week. Does anyone other than Isaac know anything about St. Monica?"

I wasn't the only one amused. Isaac and Joseph were known as the smart ones in the group. No one seemed to mind. They were some of the oldest members, and it never felt as though either was showing off. Isaac raised his hand with a defiant look at Ruth. He was clearly giving his sister a hard time only to play along. She pretended not to notice his hand in the air as she glanced around at the rest of us.

The only thing I knew about St. Monica was that she was the mother of St. Augustine. I was content to let someone else provide that information, which Jessica eventually did.

"Yes," Ruth said. "She prayed for his conversion many years before he finally became a Christian. I guess she's a model for continuing to pray even when something seems like a lost cause but also waiting for things to happen in God's time. Mostly though, she's a parent. That's what, um…" She stopped and looked at Gabriel for help.

"We thought she could be a jumping off point for talking about our parents, but Ruth was afraid it might turn into complaining about our parents."

"Ha." Isaac laughed. "I'm so going to tell Mom that you can't talk about her without complaining."

"That's not what I…" Ruth frowned at Gabriel. His comment had apparently not been the help she'd been looking for. "I didn't necessarily think it would turn into a bunch of complaining," she said. "I just wondered how we could make sure we kept the conversation productive. So anyway… the first question is…" She looked at her phone and began to read. "How has your relationship with your parents changed since becoming an adult? Specifically, how do you continue to follow the commandment to honor your parents when you no longer need to do everything they say?"

I looked around the room to see if anyone had something interesting to contribute. I only saw people looking back at me.

Jessica was the first to venture into the silence. "I will go ahead and admit I had a little trouble with that one," she said. "When I first started college, it seemed like every time I talked to either of my parents, they'd say something like, 'Make sure you're getting enough sleep,' or 'Don't wait until the last minute to start on that paper.' And then I would do the opposite just because I could. Luckily, it didn't take me too long to figure out that I was the only one who suffered when I didn't follow the advice and that that's what it was… advice. They weren't threatening to punish me or anything. They were just showing concern for my well-being, and it's not so terrible to have people care about me."

"Well, of course you take the parent side now," Eric joked, gesturing to the baby in her arms.

She smiled smugly. "Oh, yeah, parents know everything."

"I think our parents made it easy," Isaac said. "I think they just naturally shifted to asking us to do things rather than telling us around the time we were old enough we didn't have to listen." He looked at Ruth with an expression that asked if she agreed with his assessment.

I didn't hear what Ruth said because I was distracted by the realization that Isaac had nailed what Lauren was doing wrong. She asked Jessilynn and Abigail to do things, made it sound as though they had a choice, then got mad when they didn't choose what she wanted. But how did you tell kids they had to do what you said, because really they could choose to disobey no matter how you worded it? Maybe I needed to put aside the marriage books and start reading about kids. And maybe that could wait until I had a relationship that was even a little promising.

"Maybe Joseph and I were more mature than you were," Isaac said. Then he stuck his tongue out at Ruth.

"My mom still *tells* me what to do," Sebastian said. "But she uses this smug tone that says she knows I don't have to do what she says but I will as soon as I realize she's right."

I cringed. Sebastian looked amused, but that sounded super annoying to me. I couldn't remember the last time my parents told or asked me to do anything. Our relationship had gotten a bit distant for advice.

"Oh, are we talking about parents today?" Emily asked as she entered the room.

Her question wasn't immediately answered as Joseph was of course with her and several people called out birthday greetings, which made Ruth begin a chorus of the birthday song she'd promised. Though I sang quietly, I did join in and enjoyed a few moments of unity with the group. Joseph and Isaac thanked everyone before insisting we get back to the discussion.

The rest of the meeting went pretty well. I heard some great comments. I also spent a fair amount of time observing those two young women. I didn't know their names because I'd missed their arrival. Ruth had gotten some introductions when I was talking to Eric and Heather, but I'd been only vaguely aware it was happening. They definitely seemed to be there to check out the guys.

I could see them ruling out the ones who were attached based on the glances and confirming whispers. Sebastian got more glances than the others and more animated whispers. I guessed they'd gotten the same background on him as I had. It was strange to think he must be a completely different person when he was angry. I just couldn't picture him hurting anyone. But I really didn't know him well, and guys like that seemed to be pretty good at hiding the violent side.

By the time we were finishing up, I knew the newcomers had identified Eric as the most eligible bachelor in the room. They marched his way less than subtly as we began moving to leave. I quickly backed to a corner so I wouldn't have to watch anything that looked like flirting. Heather joined me.

I looked over her shoulder to make sure the group wasn't leaving the room a mess. Gabriel, Ruth, Ella and Sebastian were moving chairs and unfolding tables. It seemed obvious to me that Ella was helping because Ruth was and that Sebastian was helping because Ella was. Emily was probably right that I'd be wasting my time chasing him whether he was a good catch or not. I kept my voice low to address Heather as I put on my coat. "I think Sebastian is interested in Ella. Do you think someone should warn her about him?"

Heather snorted. "Please. That girl is scared of her own shadow. There's no way she'd let herself be alone with any guy, let alone Sebastian Jones."

I nodded uncertainly. It bothered me that Heather thought Ella's shyness was something to mock. Then again, Ella had grown up in Andauk, which meant she probably knew the story on Sebastian better than I did.

"Julia! Wait!"

We were about to slip through the doorway when I heard Ruth calling me back. When I turned around, she waved me towards her. Heather followed me.

"Can I ask you a favor?" Ruth said. "Could you maybe drop the key off at Mrs. Donnelly's for us?" She motioned to Gabriel.

He pulled the key from his pocket, but there was clear surprise on his face. This was not something they had discussed.

"I guess so," I said. I took the key from Gabriel because it didn't seem like a difficult request – I knew they just dropped it in her mailbox – and I figured it was Gabriel and not me who should be suspicious of her motives. "Where does she live?"

"Oh, it's really close, and you know what…" She paused for a moment, and I almost believed the thought was just occurring to her. "Eric came with us tonight so if you give him a ride home, he can show you on the way."

I turned to Eric because Ruth pointed at him. Eric was looking at us because he heard his name. Those new women were disappearing through the doorway. Sebastian and Ella were pushing chairs against the table farthest from us. I heard Heather laugh, and it looked like Gabriel rolled his eyes as he quickly bent forward to pull out the legs on a table. I seemed to be aware of everything except the trap I'd just walked into.

But I didn't want anyone to know I felt trapped. I smiled and said, "Okay," like it was no big deal. It wasn't really. Eric and I were friends. I could give him a ride while doing a favor for another friend. It only seemed like a big deal because I knew sitting in my car with Eric was going to make me stupid. I would be flushed and giddy and the feelings I usually controlled would be trying to control me with a bubbling, swirling mess in my stomach.

"Have fun!" Heather said as she waved goodbye.

Her comment was nearly as out of place as her smirking expression. I couldn't help rolling my eyes at her, but I still waved back.

Holding the key meant I had to be the last one out. That wasn't a problem as the others had the room ready to go. Eric and I trailed behind the other four in silence. Things were already beginning to swirl and bubble, and it wasn't limited to my stomach. I pointed to my car as soon as I locked the door. Though I thought he already knew. Gabriel's car was distinctive because it was so old, and Sebastian parked much farther from the door. There were small mounds of snow scattered around the edges of the parking lot. The bright lights made the space stand out from the surrounding darkness. Then Eric and I seemed to separate from the rest of the world as we shut ourselves into the tiny space of my car.

I made a concerted effort to ignore the stupid and put my mind to a friendly conversation. "So where does Mrs. Donnelly live?"

"Left out of the church lot," Eric said, "then right on Lakota Street."

"Got it," I said, shifting into drive. "What made you come with Gabriel and Ruth tonight?"

"And Ella," Eric said. "We were all at my parents' house for dinner, and it seemed wrong to take three cars to the same very close place. I'll actually need you to drop me at their place to get my car."

I nodded. I didn't know the math of four people and three cars. I also didn't know where Eric's parents lived any more than I knew were he lived. First we needed to find Mrs. Donnelly's house. I continued to concentrate on small talk. "You eat with your parents a lot, don't you?"

I caught a shrug out of the corner of my eye. "It's not a regular thing," Eric said. "Every now and then my mom gets the idea we need a family dinner and calls us over. I never say no when someone offers to cook for me."

One of those giddy feelings tried to make a mental note that Eric wouldn't say no if I offered to cook for him, but that was information I was never going to need.

"Right here," Eric said.

I hit the brakes kind of hard to make the turn. "Sorry. I thought we had one more block to go." We were driving away from my house so I didn't know the streets as well in that direction.

"Fourth house on the left," Eric said, pointing through the windshield. "Number 207."

I had dropped the key in a cup holder between us when we got in the car. Eric picked it up by its light blue key chain as I pulled into the driveway. "I'll run it up to the house," he said.

It made sense to me that the person in the passenger seat should be the one to get out while the engine was still running. I wrapped my head around that idea to keep out any fuzzy ideas of chivalry. Eric glanced at me right before he got out of the car though. His eyes pierced my tightly wrapped mind to let me know he was happy to do even this small thing for me. The knowledge touched a mushy spot but also something worse, something I didn't want to acknowledge, something that made me feel for a brief moment that Eric wasn't the one doing something wrong.

The blast of cold air before he shut the door allowed me to clear my head. I calmly observed as he jogged up Mrs. Donnelly's porch steps. He opened the mailbox and dropped the key. The front door burst open before he got off the porch. A middle-aged woman stood in the doorway pulling a cardigan closed as she addressed Eric.

I recognized Mrs. Donnelly even though I'd never spoken to her. Two different people had pointed her out to me as someone to avoid because she was always recruiting volunteers for something at the church. I'd heard it was impossible to say no to her, and Eric was nodding. She moved her glasses down the bridge of her nose to look at him over the frames. Everything about the situation said that Eric was cornered, except the fact that Mrs. Donnelly was in the doorway and he had a ton of open space behind him.

After a few moments, she disappeared into the house. Eric stayed on the porch. He turned towards me and held up a finger to indicate he needed a minute. I smiled, mostly to myself because I didn't know if he could see me through the dark windshield. I wondered if he was still happy he was the one who got out of the car. I might be forced to remind him he volunteered to take the key when he told me what job she stuck him with.

Mrs. Donnelly returned to the doorway and handed Eric a piece of paper. There was a bit more nodding, then he waved as he left the porch and she went back inside.

I felt another wave of cold air as Eric reclaimed the passenger seat. He set the paper in his lap as he reached for the seatbelt. It looked as though he'd acquired a different key as well. He turned to me with an apologetic expression.

I really hadn't minded waiting an extra minute. I thought it was funny that he got roped into something. I tried not to look too amused by it as I asked, "What does she want you to do?"

"Well, apparently she got a call this evening from the woman who is in charge of washing the altar server robes. She was going to pick them up tonight but had some kind of car trouble. Mrs. Donnelly assured her that it would not be a problem because she was expecting Gabriel Chadwick to stop by shortly. Since he is such a caring and dependable young man, she knew he could be counted on to help in this time of need." Eric sighed. "I believe that was the point in the conversation when she realized I was *not* Gabriel."

"Oh, my goodness." The playful annoyance on his face made me laugh so hard. I noticed the strong family resemblance, but I still couldn't believe people actually mixed them up. Eric didn't wear glasses, and his jaw was a little less square. Their eyes were the same striking shade of blue, but Eric's were far more... none of the adjectives that came to mind were objective. It was really best not to think about his eyes except to say they were blue. Blue was a fact.

Eric continued, "So she shifted to saying that she knew I enjoyed being helpful at least as much as my brother so of course I wouldn't mind doing this small task."

"Of course not," I said. "That's pretty impressive that she was able to turn flattery into sibling rivalry."

"Without missing a beat," Eric said. "The woman is a pro."

We shared a laugh until something he said caught up with me. "Wait. She asked you to do it tonight? As in, right now?"

He nodded. "I guess the robes are supposed to be washed and ironed and back at the church in time for a wedding at one o'clock tomorrow so she wants to be able to start first thing in the morning."

That sounded reasonable. And it was nice of Eric to volunteer, whether he'd been strong-armed or not. But I was driving. If he'd volunteered for an errand right now, he'd volunteered me, too.

12

The paper Eric was holding had an address scribbled on it. I couldn't make it out from my side of the car. "Where are we going?" I asked.

His eyes widened in surprise for only a moment before he said, "First back to the church, then somewhere on Farber Road. That's a mile or so outside of town. I'll have to look up the specific address." He already had his phone out to do that bit of research.

I turned the car around because the first part was easy. "I have no idea where Farber Road is," I admitted. "You'll be in charge of directions after we leave the church."

"Yeah." He sounded distracted, then I could tell he was nodding. "Yeah. This shouldn't be hard to find."

Neither of us said anything else before I parked in front of St. Jude's. It only took a minute, but that was enough time for something to build up between us. I wasn't sure how to describe it. This errand, however simple the actual task, would be a shared experience unlike Eric showing up where I worked or both of us showing up for a meeting. It triggered a sense of newness or expectation or... some other feeling I didn't want to examine.

Eric got out of the car, and I followed him up the front steps of the church. He held the door for me to go in first. It was dark and still inside. I loved empty churches because I knew they weren't empty. God's presence felt more real, almost tangible, when there weren't other people around to distract me. Peace replaced that unsettled feeling that had been building in the car.

As Eric passed me to lead the way to the sacristy, I had an inexplicable urge to take hold of his hand to make him walk slowly with me. Fortunately, I was in control of my impulses and not the other way around. I walked a few steps behind him.

He unlocked the room and went straight to a closet like he knew what he was doing. I reminded myself that he had been an altar server at this church. Somewhere between fifteen and twenty robes hung in the closet. That surprised me since I'd never seen more than three or four servers at a Mass. But I could tell by the lengths that there were a lot of different sizes so the quantity made sense as soon as I had a few seconds to think about it.

"Mrs. Donnelly said to take the hangers, too," Eric said as he reached in. He put one arm on either side and squished all the robes together at the base of the hangers, then tried to lift them off the bar all at once. It didn't quite work. Most of the hangers came off, but there were at least two in the middle still hooked on the bar. Eric didn't have any free hands to move them. He looked at me for help.

The uncertainty in his expression made me laugh, which he didn't seem to appreciate. I reached under his arm and over the robes to get to the hangers. The awkward position necessitated some contact between my shoulder and Eric's chest. I tried really hard not to notice. But I'm mentioning it so obviously I noticed. Stupid hormones. Stupid blushing. I concentrated on getting my fingers under the hangers so I could lift the remaining hooks and extricate myself from the proximity as fast as I could. Eric let me get out of the way before he tipped the stack sideways to drape over his right arm with the left balancing it.

I left the room first and turned back to wait for Eric to relock it.

"Um…" He bit the side of his lip. "I think I need help again."

His hands were too full to lock the door. I just stared at him though, possibly with my mouth open, while I fought off a terrifying picture of me fishing in his pocket for the key. Was I strong enough to hold all of those robes? They looked somewhat precarious to transfer, but I definitely preferred that to the alternative.

"If you could just…" Eric nodded towards his outstretched arms. There was a faint clinking sound.

I realized with much relief that the key was still in his hand. It was just buried under some sleeves. "No problem," I said. I shifted the fabric around until I found his hand and took the key out of it. I tried the handle after I turned the key to make sure it was locked, then I absently twisted the chain around my finger and off again as we returned to the church exit.

Eric pushed the door open with his back and held it for me with his foot even though he was carrying an armload of robes and I was carrying a few keys.

I opened the door to the backseat of my car for him. "The backseat doesn't get much use," I said, "so I hope it's pretty clean in there."

Eric was leaning over trying to get the stack of robes onto the seat so his voice was muffled. "I'm not sure it matters too much if they're about to be washed."

I only nodded, which he probably couldn't see. I didn't want to point out that I was more concerned about what Eric thought of my car than what the robes thought of it.

He folded the ends over so nothing stuck out before he closed the door. Then he looked at me thoughtfully. "Let's return the key first so we don't forget, then drop off the robes. Does that sound like a plan to you?"

"Do you mean does it sound like a *good* plan?"

His eyes darted to the side at me being difficult on purpose, but he did smile, too. "Yes," he said.

I nodded again and gestured to the car. I was anxious to get back inside and turn on the heater.

Eric deposited the second key in Mrs. Donnelly's mailbox without being stopped again. He blew out a quick breath as though he'd dodged a bullet. Then he pointed up the street. "Right at the stoplight, then we'll head straight about a mile and a half before we hit Farber Road."

"Got it," I said, checking my rearview.

"So, um, you haven't mentioned your family recently," Eric said. "Have you seen them since Christmas?"

I shook my head. "No, but my mom actually just invited everyone for dinner on Sunday. Here's hoping for a dearth of meltdowns."

"A dearth?" Eric repeated. "Not the first time I've been impressed with your vocabulary."

"Well, I... work at a library," I said, as though I obviously absorbed words by osmosis. I couldn't think of anything better to say when I was embarrassed by his flattery. I could tell it was sincere.

"I know," he said, "and how is work going, by the way?"

"I have to do storytime on Monday."

Eric was quiet for a few moments before he said, "Okay. I'm confused. You say that like it's some kind of punishment, but I thought you wanted a chance to do storytime."

"I do. I just..." I wanted to tell him about it so badly, but I knew if I even cracked the floodgate, I'd tell him *everything* about it. That's why I was hesitating.

"Do you know what books you're going to read?" His show of interest threw the gate wide open.

"Sort of. I picked out too many books so I could put aside the ones that weren't good enough. But I ended up eliminating all of them and then I had to try to figure out which ones would be okay after all but I can't do voices. I tried so many different ways to make my voice sound like different characters and it always sounds the same. I even tried holding a cup in front of my mouth to talk into it and it was so dumb and…" I paused only long enough to get a breath. "I even thought about wearing a costume to distract the kids from my reading because I was stumbling over easy words. I even had trouble turning the pages because of nerves in my fingers and that was when I was sitting in my own house without an audience." I finished with a deeper breath. It felt so good to share my frustrations, I wasn't even worried about being mocked for them.

"I think I would like to see you dressed as a fairy," Eric said.

That made me laugh. Not only had Eric not laughed at me, but he'd gotten me laughing at myself. "A fairy?" I asked.

"Sure," he said. "What did you have in mind?"

I shrugged. "I didn't really have anything in mind. I just had a vague idea of some sort of story lady costume I could wear each time. But it might be months before I get to do it again anyway – longer if I bomb – so the kids won't remember."

"They'd remember a fairy," Eric said. I was watching the road, but I could hear the teasing smile in his voice. "Put some tinsel in your hair and a pair of wings. Story fairy."

"I put away my Christmas stuff, and I don't have any wings. What's your real advice?"

"You want real advice?"

"Yes."

"Um… hang on. I think our turn is coming up."

I took my foot off the gas while he scanned the flat barren landscape.

"Yeah," he said. "Turn right where that other car is coming out."

That advice was easy to follow. I waited to see if he had anything to offer regarding my storytime stress out.

"Well, I, um… you know how some people say, 'You're trying too hard,' and they mean it in a bad way?"

"Yeah?"

"I think…" Eric said. "Well, I think maybe that doesn't apply in this case."

"It doesn't?"

"Yeah. I mean, no, it doesn't." Eric was looking out the side window.

It was a quiet street with no other headlights in sight and very few houses. I slowed down to make the numbers on the mailboxes easier to read.

"Twenty-two forty-seven," he reminded me.

I nodded, though I was still trying to figure out how to politely tell him that his terrible advice didn't even make sense.

The numbers skipped ahead so that our destination was suddenly upon us. I pulled into the driveway, shifted to park and turned to Eric. "The only help you're going to give me is to tell me advice that *doesn't* apply?"

He smiled at my sarcastic tone, but there was something sheepish in his eyes. "Yes, I… Well, I've heard people say that kids know when someone is just going through the motions. Maybe the most important thing is that they believe you want to be there sharing the stories with them. I think if you can give them that… the rest might not be so important."

"You think so?"

He shrugged somewhat helplessly. "Either that or bring sock puppets."

I laughed again.

"I'll be right back," he said as he opened his door.

A glance at the backseat told me the robes were no longer stacked. They had slid around, and the hangers had fallen inside some of them. I got out to help. I walked around to the passenger side and held my arms out. "Load me up with a few, then you can get the rest easier."

He nodded and pulled out a handful of robes. He draped them over my arms. The rest he wadded into his arms like a load of laundry. That was probably not a bad thing since we were delivering laundry.

Eric walked ahead of me and managed to push the doorbell with his elbow. It must have been loud because I heard the brief melody from the porch.

A cute old woman answered the door. She was around four and a half feet tall with white hair, rosy cheeks, and a friendly smile. "Oh, you kids are lifesavers," she said.

"Hello, Mrs. McGrady," Eric said. "Where do you want these?"

She stepped back to hold the door wide. "Come inside, and I'll show you." She closed the door behind us and led us to the back of her house. There she opened a frosted glass door to the most spacious laundry room I'd ever seen. There was only one washer and dryer. There was also a deep sink and two ironing boards next to a few other tools I didn't recognize. She had a shelf full of different bottles where I would have only had my one bottle of some generic brand of soap.

"Just drop everything on that table there." The woman pointed.

Eric deposited his load, then relieved me of mine to set on top.

"Are you going to be able to get these back to the church tomorrow without a problem, Mrs. McGrady?" he asked.

"Oh, yes." She waved away his offer of help before he could finish making it. "My husband is out of town tonight, but he'll be back in the morning and then I can take his car."

"Okay. We'll get out of your way them." Eric exited the laundry room to return to the front door.

I followed closely, wondering why I felt the need to stick to him when there was nothing remotely threatening about the nice woman.

"Thank you both so much for your help," she said at the door.

"You're welcome," Eric said simply. He motioned for me to go out first.

I gave the woman a friendly smile as I left.

As she returned it, her eyes darted to Eric and back with a small nod of approval.

I turned quickly towards the driveway so she wouldn't see me looking disgusted. The approval implied that I had chosen him as more than a friend. Running an errand with a guy did not mean there was something going on between us. Ruth and Mrs. Donnelly were the ones responsible for my current situation. I hadn't chosen it.

The car hadn't completely cooled when we returned to it. Eric asked if I needed directions back.

"Well, I guess we're headed to your parents' house now, and I don't know where that is so feel free to offer suggestions."

He smiled.

I turned the car towards Andauk since he did not suggest otherwise.

"I hear you've been to Burger Brothers," Eric said.

I felt my chest tighten. I was afraid he was about to ask me about being there with Sean. "Um… Burger Brothers? What do you mean?"

"Ruth was telling us earlier tonight about how Emily got Chip to make something not on the menu," Eric said. "She had us cracking up, and my dad was so jealous. He's always trying to get Chip to make him a burger that's less well done, and Chip just pretends he doesn't hear him."

"Oh, right." I smiled and relaxed. "He did not seem pleased with her request, but… man, those shakes were good."

"Are you going to try to get him to make you another one sometime?"

"Ha. I'm not that brave," I said. "I think I would like to send Emily in to get me one to go. Then he wouldn't know it was for me the next time I ate there."

Eric chuckled at my admission of cowardice. "But you'd like to eat there again?"

"Of course," I said, too quickly. "Things that are on the menu are delicious, too." My answer was hasty because I realized while I was still speaking that his question had a leading tone. And where it was leading. He was building up to asking me to go to Burger Brothers with him. Even if we classified it as a friendly meal, it would feel like a date to me because of what I felt when he was with me. That would be bad.

"What street do your parents live on?" I asked. Yes, it was a distraction. It was also information that I would honestly need in the near future.

"Uh, Waterford Way."

"Where is that?"

When he tried to explain, I didn't recognize the first cross street he mentioned. Or the second. By the time I knew where I was going, Eric was teasing me about how often I must get lost. I assured him that I knew all the streets I needed to know and just didn't memorize maps in my free time. I hadn't lived in Andauk nearly as long as he had after all.

The light conversation lasted until I was stopping my car behind his in front of a house on Waterford Way. I couldn't tell if he'd been aware that I redirected the topic on purpose, if he forgot he was trying to ask me something, or if maybe he'd simply chickened out. Whatever a gift horse was, I was looking anywhere but its mouth.

"Here we are," I said.

"Thanks for the ride," Eric said. He didn't put his hand on the door handle. "I know it ended up being a lot longer than you expected."

"Well, it was longer than you expected, too." I smiled to remember him standing on Mrs. Donnelly's porch looking trapped.

"Yeah, but I totally expected you to drop me off here to deal with the chore on my own. So, thanks."

We'd clearly established that my geography was less than exemplary, but I was pretty sure we were no more than a quarter mile from Mrs. Donnelly's house. I could have dropped Eric off to volunteer by himself. Why hadn't I thought to do that?

"You made it not a chore at all," Eric said. He held out his hand like he wanted me to shake it.

I was too startled to do anything other than accept the offer.

He didn't exactly shake my hand, just held it for a few moments while he said, "Thanks again. I'll see you soon."

I watched him move quickly from my car to his. The lights came on as he started it. I followed his car until I got to my turn. I tried not to think or feel much of anything after I got home. If I thought too much about what was happening with Eric, I'd know it wasn't good. And if I felt too much, I might be happy about it.

13

It was a dark and stormy afternoon. Well, it was dark anyway. The heavily overcast sky gave credence to the predictions of a snowy night. Lillian was keeping a close eye on the weather. She lived a bit out of town and was prepared to close the library early if the roads might be slick before she made it home safely.

It didn't come to that. I left right on time knowing that she would text me if we'd be closed or opening late the following day. I liked my job, but I still felt the excitement of a kid hoping for a snow day.

There were a few flurries in the air as I walked up my front sidewalk. I made it onto the porch before Snowflake, which was unusual. I grabbed the mail from the box. Two advertisements and nothing more interesting. Where was my cat? I looked around and called out for her. There was no meowing response, no streak of movement across the front yard.

I opened the door and held it for a minute. I still expected her to come running inside. When she didn't, I knew I needed to do something. I couldn't continue my normal routine as though Snowflake wasn't part of it. I went inside and put down everything but my keys and my phone, which I stuffed into either pocket of my coat. I switched from my dress shoes to a pair of boots and wrapped a scarf around my neck. Then I went outside to search.

I didn't have a very specific plan other than to start walking. I thought Snowflake would recognize me on foot and come to me, hopefully within a few blocks of my house. Beyond that, I didn't know what to do. I only knew I was way too restless to sit still. The snow began to fall in force as I locked my door, almost as though turning the key had been the cue.

It was cold enough that the snow stayed frozen and bounced off me rather than soaking into my coat. The wind was calm, letting it fall straight down. But there was still so much of it that I had trouble seeing very far ahead. I would definitely need to count on Snowflake finding me. I turned the first corner because I figured circles would keep me closer to my house than a straight line. I saw another person on the other side of the street who appeared to be jogging. What crazy person was out jogging in a blizzard?

The other person crossed the street and seemed to be headed straight for me. I slowed my steps, trying to figure out if I recognized him. I did. Gabriel Chadwick was the crazy person jogging in a blizzard.

He apparently recognized me as well. "Hi, Julia." He stopped in front of me.

"Hi," I said.

"Is something wrong?" he asked. It seemed he was more concerned about me being out in bad weather than himself.

"My cat is missing," I said.

"Oh, dear." He looked around us. "Do you think maybe she just took shelter somewhere?"

"Maybe," I said, more because I liked the idea than really hoped it was true. "She should have come home before it started though."

"Do you want me to help you look?"

"Oh, that's nice, but... I don't want to put you out."

He shrugged. "I just started my run so I'll be out here for a while. There's no reason I can't keep my eyes open for a cat at the same time. What does she look like?"

I pulled out my phone to show him a picture. I was glad it took me a minute because it would have been embarrassing to discover that all of my pictures were of my cat. "Here." I held it up. "Her name is Snowflake."

His eyebrows wrinkled under the knit cap on his head. "Snowflake?"

"Yeah, I know. I named her when I was a teenager. I thought I was being clever or ironic or something." Snowflake was not a white cat. She had gray and black stripes.

"Will she come to me if I call her?"

"Probably," I said. "She's real friendly. Even likes kids."

He nodded and looked as though he was about to continue on his way. "Hey, do you mind if I recruit anyone I think might help?"

"I guess not."

"Okay," Gabriel said. "Good luck."

"Thanks." I wasn't sure if he heard my gratitude as he'd already started jogging away. I was tempted to jog a bit myself to warm up. I'd begun to shiver in the minute I stopped to talk. I wasn't much of a jogger though. I picked up my pace, hoping a brisk walk would get the blood pumping enough.

"Snowflake." It wasn't much of a call. My voice sounded timid and shaky because I didn't want to catch the attention of anyone other than my cat. Where was she?

I thought about what Gabriel had said about her seeking shelter. That really was possible. Sometimes animals seemed to know when bad weather was approaching. She might have hunkered down somewhere, ready to come home as soon as the snow cleared.

It was also true that she was super friendly. If someone was playing with her, she might not realize it was time to come home. I would particularly understand her losing track of time if someone had fed her. Not that cats could tell time. But she wouldn't have an empty stomach urging her back to me. Every time thoughts of cars or larger animals entered my head, I challenged myself to come up with another happy reason she was late, only late.

Enough snow had fallen that I was leaving footprints on the sidewalk. That encouraged me, too. I scanned the ground as I walked and couldn't see any animal tracks. I imagined they were all hunkered down somewhere. After several aimless circles, I had to admit I needed to do the same. My fingers were numb inside my gloves, and the snow was stinging my face. Once I acknowledged the cold, I couldn't escape it fast enough.

I hugged myself as I hurried home. I stripped off my bundling and made a very hot bowl of soup for dinner. My fingers burned as the feeling returned, but my stomach felt better with food. I kept glancing at Snowflake's empty food dish. I couldn't stop myself from thinking about how hard it was to never know what happened to my first cat. I used to imagine that she somehow lost her collar and got adopted by a very nice family who thought she was a stray. I didn't want to do that again.

I didn't turn on the TV or any music after dinner. I sat with a book I wasn't really reading while I watched the window for the snow to stop and listened for meowing at my door. The snow continued to fall thickly. Silence was all I heard outside. Until there was a knock so sharp I jumped and almost dropped my book. I grabbed a tissue and hastily wiped my eyes on my way to the front window. It was Snowflake!

Obviously, she hadn't knocked on the door. But she was right outside, wrapped protectively in the arms of someone who told me he was not a cat person.

I flung the door open and smiled at both of them. "Hi. You found her!"

Eric tipped his head in deference. "I can only take credit for bringing her home, and she probably would have done that on her own eventually."

My curiosity and my eagerness to avoid any further chills that night made me wave him inside so I could close the door. I pulled my cat from his arms into mine. Her fur was cold as I nuzzled my face against her. Snowflake wasn't interested in a lengthy reunion though. She quickly wiggled to be put down. I obliged and turned to Eric. "How did you end up with her?"

"Well… I guess you bumped into Gabriel and mentioned that she was missing so he recognized the cat his neighbor was playing with when he got home. He didn't know how to contact you so he called Ruth, who told him to call me."

I nodded as I got my head around that line of events.

"I figured the cat would find its way back to you soon, but given the weather and Gabriel said you looked worried…" Eric trailed off as he seemed to be looking for the right words to ask if it was okay that he'd cut me off before I could start crying in earnest and saved me from a night of worry.

"Thank you for bringing her home," I said. "Really. Thank you."

"My pleasure. I hope you weren't out looking for her for too long?"

"Maybe longer than I should have." I flexed my fingers to remind myself that they were back to normal. "I haven't felt so close to frostbite since I used to play in the snow as a kid."

Eric looked down at my hands as though checking for himself that they had recovered.

It made me remember the recent night when he had held my hand, however briefly, before getting out of the car. The gesture still confused me. It hadn't been overtly romantic. It had seemed a deliberate effort to spark some familiarity. And I'd been too surprised to stop it. I distracted myself from those thoughts by watching Snowflake. She was rubbing her face on my furniture as though she needed to reclaim her territory after being gone a couple extra hours.

"Uh, so… while I'm here…" Eric started.

For some reason, the hesitation didn't make me nervous. I didn't jump in to redirect.

"Can I ask how your first storytime went?" he said. "I was thinking about you this morning."

"I think it went pretty well." I smiled self-consciously. As soon as I got through it, I started to realize I'd been silly to let myself get so worked up. But Eric wasn't looking at me as though I'd been silly. He was asking with real interest, clearly expecting me to say a lot more.

"I was still so nervous this morning, I thought about asking Lillian if I could have another week to prepare. Then I figured that would only give me another week to freak out. And Lillian showed up five minutes before I had to start anyway. I said a quick prayer on my way into the room and dove in. I started with the book I thought was funniest, and the kids laughed. A lot. When I stamped their hands afterward, only one girl asked why I was reading instead of Miss Lillian."

"She probably didn't mean any offense," Eric said.

"No. I know she didn't. She was one of the older kids but still couldn't have been more than five. She was only curious, and even

147

if she was asking because she likes Lillian better I... Well, I don't know how to explain me suddenly coming to my senses."

"About?" Eric looked confused and – surprisingly – still interested.

That gave me the incentive to explain better. "I guess once I proved to myself that I could do it – the kids seemed to like all the books I picked – I stopped comparing myself to Lillian. I realized I could be good even if I'm not *as* good. I can admire Lillian's performances without being envious."

"And what did she think?" he asked. "Was she watching or listening to you read?"

I nodded. "I didn't see her, but she must have been at least listening because she told me later that I did great." Now I was bordering on bragging. But Lillian was the master. If she could say I'd done even okay without condescension, then I could feel pride in a job well done. Regardless of how much anxiety had preceded it.

Eric smiled at my new enthusiasm.

"And..." I paused to make sure he was still listening to the biggest news. "She said I should do all the Monday storytimes from now on, and she'll only do Thursdays."

"Congratulations! That's kind of like a promotion. I bet you're already planning future weeks."

"Oh, yeah." I held one arm over the other. "I have a list of books this long, and I'm working to divide them into other lists like how long they are and which ones are funny mostly because of the pictures because those will be better when I have a smaller group for the kids to see, and the books that have surprises so I don't use those all at once, and also by main characters so I don't do all bunnies unless that's an intentional theme. And I've been thinking more about a costume."

"You really want to wear a costume?"

"Nothing elaborate," I said. "But the kids got a little excited as soon as I came in because they knew it was time to start, and I thought maybe if I had a funny hat or something that I only wear during storytime... that might announce the start more dramatically than simply walking in."

Eric tipped his head. "Fairy wings?"

I laughed. "I've actually considered that. Wings would be easy to slip on and off while I'm at work. But they'd have to be some pretty cool wings."

"Of course," Eric said. "Maybe with lights?"

"Wow. Do you think I could find some that light up?"

He only shrugged.

"Well, I want to think about it for a while to be sure I'll like something before I commit to wearing it every Monday."

"Makes sense." Eric glanced out the window. "I should probably get going. It'll be a slow drive home."

"Oh, right." I stepped to the window and pulled aside the curtain. Several inches of snow had fallen, and my street hadn't been plowed. I felt a surge of worry, not so much for Eric's safety – I trusted him to be careful – but because I reminded myself of the reason he was braving those streets. He did it for me. "You'll... be okay?" I asked.

"Yeah. It's not that far." He didn't sound concerned. "If I get stuck or slide off the road, I'll just walk home and get some guys to help me push it out in the morning." He put his hand on the door but didn't open it.

I thought he might be bracing himself for the cold. It turned out to be something else entirely.

He let go of the handle and looked me right in the eye. "Will you meet me for dinner some night this week?"

My stupid heart jumped at the invitation, which was why I

knew it was a bad idea. Emotions did not get to lead. Rejecting the impulse to agree was easier than finding the words to reject it out loud. "I... uh... I don't know."

"I thought Friday would work since we could go straight to the church after, but if you'd rather get together on your day off, we could meet on Wednesday."

I had to look away. My eyes landed on Snowflake, curled up on my couch, more comfortable than I was.

"What's wrong, Julia?"

I could only shake my head. I thought Eric would ask me out eventually, but I didn't think it would be so hard to turn him down. I hadn't expected him to wait so long.

"I've been visiting you at the library for like six months," he said, apparently reading my mind on the time that had passed. "I thought, especially after you went with me to Mrs. McGrady's on Friday... I thought you wouldn't mind a change of venue now and then."

"That was a mistake," I blurted.

He wrinkled his eyes. "What was?"

"I thought... I thought I had to go because I was driving. I didn't think that... that your car was right around the corner."

"Are you saying you would have ditched me if it had occurred to you?"

"No, I..." I definitely wouldn't have put it like that anyway. I could not get my mind into the conversation. I knew I had to tell Eric to leave, but a confusion of feelings was clawing at me, trying to get my attention.

"Julia, I... Do you really want to get to know me better or are you just stalling until I give up? Tell me straight up if you don't want to see me anymore."

I saw it only as an opportunity to escape the charged moment. "That might be best," I said.

Eric hadn't expected that. He'd asked me to say it, and yet it clearly took him by surprise. His mouth moved soundlessly and his eyes seemed to droop. Finally, he gave a quick nod of understanding and jerked the door open. He had almost closed it behind himself when he poked his head through.

I would have leaped at a second chance.

He only said, "I was supposed to tell you that Jojo fed the cat. I don't know how much he gave her." Then he closed the door.

14

Trying not to think about something – or someone – is time consuming. I didn't want to think about Eric. I'd been saying that for months, yet when a thought of him entered my head, I did little to chase it away. That changed in a hurry after he brought Snowflake home.

Every time he entered my head, I chastised myself with a reminder not to think about Eric, which was a thought that included Eric. It was a never-ending cycle. I might as well have been a dog chasing my tail. My head told me that turning him down was the right thing to do because it's what I'd planned to do from the day I first met him. It should have been the end of the story. But there was a page I didn't want to turn, and it was making me miserable.

I was distracted at work. I had talked to Eric in so many different sections of the library, they all made me think of him. I was distracted at home, when I thought about plans for storytime, when I pet Snowflake, when I pulled all the lists he'd sent me from a drawer and reread them.

Emily called me early Wednesday afternoon, and I was grateful for the distraction from my distraction. She immediately asked how I was doing. I said I was fine even though I wasn't. Then I asked if she and Joseph had started making wedding plans.

"Two weeks from Monday," she said.

"You're getting married in two weeks!?" My grip tightened on the phone to keep from dropping it.

"No, no, no." Emily was laughing. "That's our first meeting with the pastor, when we'll start trying to schedule some pre-wedding stuff and eventually a date for the ceremony."

"That makes more sense," I said. She'd certainly drawn my attention from Eric when I thought she was planning a wedding so quickly. Except, of course, when I thought about how she'd drawn my attention from Eric. "What did your parents say when you told them?"

"They might have been even more excited than I expected, especially my mom. My dad was mostly grilling me about Joseph as though he hasn't already asked me a ton of questions to make sure I'm sure. But my mom was like… Well, I could tell she was jumping up and down through the phone. Until she was crying, which was ridiculous."

"She was crying?" I asked. "You mean happy crying, right?"

"Like crazy. I asked her if she'd want to stand up as a matron of honor – or maybe call her an official witness because we're going for an old fashioned wedding – and she asked if I wouldn't rather ask one of my friends, but she could hardly get the words out because she was gasping for air." Emily sounded exasperated at the display of emotion. "I couldn't take it back then if I'd wanted to. Okay, Mom, I'll just get Julia to do it while you get control of yourself. I mean, you or any of my friends would be happy if I asked, but it wouldn't mean so much that you were overcome with tears, right?"

"No tears," I said. I would have considered it an honor, especially given that I'd only known Emily a few months, but I was not prone to bursting into tears. "What do you mean by old fashioned?"

"Simple mostly. Or… well, okay, cheap. I can tell *you* that.

We're trying to keep to a modest budget. Joseph says we need to have money for the life we want and not just the day, and I totally agree with him."

I was nodding at the phone, too. That might have been the least flighty thing Emily had ever said.

"The only thing I want," she continued, "is a pretty dress. I want my wedding dress to be the prettiest dress I've ever worn, but we don't have to go real extravagant to reach that criteria. The rest... can be the bare minimum. I know my parents though. They'll be like, 'Emily, you can't have a cheap wedding.' So we're framing it as old fashioned. I think that'll help with his parents, too, because... uh, his mom has already... I think she's worried that him being exceedingly frugal is going to scare me off before the wedding, and... we can pretend old fashioned was my idea."

"Was it?"

"I don't remember who said it first, but... I know it's what we both want." Emily paused long enough that I sensed a switching of gears. "What's up with you? Enjoying your day off?"

"Eh."

"Bored?"

"Not really."

"I didn't interrupt anything, did I?"

"Oh, no. At least nothing I hadn't wanted interrupted."

"What have you been doing?"

"Trying not to think about Eric," I said. Then I winced and wished I'd been trying not to talk about him.

Emily misinterpreted my statement as a good thing. "Ooh," she said with interest. "Things went well on Friday? Ruth told me how she set you guys up."

"Friday was okay," I said, though I was grumbling on the inside at the reminder of being set up.

"Wait, I'm sensing... The way you say Friday was okay makes me think something else was not okay."

I didn't say anything at first. I wanted to tell her what happened, but I also didn't.

Emily sucked in a breath as a thought occurred to her. "Has he still not asked you out?" she asked.

"He did." The words slipped out before I decided to say them because I was surprised by her tone. It seemed to imply I was anxious for that to happen when I'd already explained to her why I wasn't.

"Well, what did you say?"

"I turned him down of course."

"And now you regret it, and that's why you can't stop thinking about him?"

"No."

"Oh," Emily said. "So when are you guys going out?"

"What?"

"What?"

I wanted to blame Emily for our conversation breaking down because she seemed the more scatterbrained of the two of us. But I knew that wouldn't be fair. I was the one trying to talk without thinking.

"I'm sorry," Emily said. "I'll just listen. Go ahead."

"Well... I saw Eric on Monday. He asked if I would have dinner with him sometime this week. I said no because... I knew that was right. But now I... I feel like something's wrong."

When I was quiet for a minute, Emily prompted me. "What's wrong?" she asked.

It was time to name the feeling I didn't want to think about. "I feel guilty."

"Because he was disappointed?"

"No. I... He made it sound like I was breaking up with him when..."

There were a few sort of squeaky noises through the phone. Emily seemed to be struggling to just listen when she didn't think I was doing enough talking. "What did he say?"

"He said I should tell him if I didn't want to see him anymore."

"Anymore?" Emily repeated.

"Yeah."

"Hmm. I'm not sure what I'm missing. I know you've technically been seeing each other most Fridays for a while, but that's not... well, it's not just you and him. You also told me you chatted when he volunteered at the library a few times. Is that it?"

"It, um, was more than a few times."

"Like... ten times?"

I didn't want to answer. I wanted her to be mad at Eric for making me feel guilty when I hadn't done anything wrong. Emily's questions seemed to be leading away from that conclusion. "I don't know," I said finally. "But more than ten."

"Okay. So he's been stopping by the library fairly regularly, often enough that you've lost count. Was it mostly just small talk or have you guys had time to really talk?"

"Sometimes all he did was put away books."

"Sometimes?"

"Yes." I was trying to sound matter-of-fact and not defensive. "Sometimes I was too busy to talk."

"Wow," Emily said. "There is more going on than the rest of us realized."

"Who exactly is *the rest of us*?"

"Oh, just the girls. I saw Ruth and Ella at the Zieberts on Sunday. That's when she told me about getting you and Eric to return the key together. She didn't seem to know anything about him showing up at the library – and I didn't tell her, by the way – and thought he only needed an opportunity away from the other Friday night group members to make a move, but..." Emily paused as though she was trying to make sense of something. "But it sounds like he's had a lot of opportunities." She still sounded confused.

"I guess," was all I said.

"Wow. I don't... Well, I wasn't there so I don't know how you two could have gotten your wires crossed for so long. Was he that subtle about... It's just... wow. Can I ask you something though? It's kind of personal," she said.

We were already talking about my love life. "Go ahead."

"I know you're trying to be all rational about finding a guy, you know, someone who looks good on paper and all that. What was it that made you rule Eric out?"

"I told you. I like him too much."

"Yeah," Emily said slowly. "I know that would make it harder to be objective, but he must have said something that – Ah!" She was cut off by a high-pitched wailing noise. "Why is that... Oh, no, smoke alarm, gotta go." She hung up on me.

I understood she had something important to deal with so I did not feel slighted by the abrupt end to the call. In fact, I was sort of relieved. I held my phone while I said a quick prayer that Emily's emergency could be handled quickly. I would try to remember to ask her about it later. A good friend showed interest in another friend's life, particularly when she might have a chance to tease her about something.

I was setting the phone down when I was startled by a thunk on my porch. It sounded like something had been dropped, but I wasn't expecting anything. A delivery truck was pulling away as I reached the window. I opened the front door and found a package. I picked it up curiously. It wasn't very heavy.

Snowflake zipped past me into the house while the door was open. I'd let her out after lunch. Apparently, she was done with the snow already. I didn't blame her. Though I did wonder how long she'd been watching for me to open the door. It was much earlier than I'd be coming home from work.

I hurried in out of the cold myself, still trying to remember if I'd ordered something. "Hey, Snowflake," I said, "have you been playing with the computer while I wasn't looking?"

Her only response was to mash her face against my ankles. That probably counted as a no.

Having given myself enough anticipation, I set the package on the table and ripped it open. I gasped when I discovered what was inside. Fairy wings. There was only one person who could have sent me fairy wings. But when? Did he order them after he suggested it on Friday or after we talked on Monday?

I tossed the wings aside and dug through the air pockets for a packing slip. I checked the date against my calendar. Monday. But there was no time listed. I hadn't talked to him until the evening, but he could have ordered them later. Monday didn't clarify anything.

Then I noticed an equally cryptic gift message at the bottom. It was only one word. Maybe? The question mark said it all. I'd received a package with no answers.

I switched my focus to what *was* in the box. The picture looked promising, silvery white wings with delicate twinkle lights. I wanted to tear open the plastic, but did I dare? If Eric had sent them before I refused his dinner invitation, which I had to admit seemed likely, then I probably shouldn't accept this gift. How would I go about returning it though? I was in luck. Closer inspection revealed little white snaps. The plastic could be opened without tearing it. I could just see what they looked like without committing to keeping them.

The fabric fluttered downward as I pulled it from the package. The wings popped open with wires along the top to hold them out while the rest of the silvery material hung free. There were straps to put my arms through like a backpack, and a small white box for batteries. I needed batteries before I tried them on.

I happened to have exactly what I needed. The lid clicked into place over the batteries, and I put my arms through the straps. I picked up one of the books I planned to read next and carried it to my bedroom where there was a full-length mirror. The lights didn't flash. They simply faded in and out at different times. They were very tiny. It didn't take much imagination to make them look like magic sparkles, like something from a fairy tale. They were beautiful. They were... perfect.

I posed in front of the mirror with the book and admired the wings until I started to cry. I finally admitted that it wasn't Eric I was trying so hard not to think about but what I'd done to him. I'd hurt him. And I'd done it on purpose.

15

"They were in the car!" Sami proclaimed. Her phone and keys made the usual racket against the desk. She'd evidently just walked in, though I hadn't seen her until she was right in front of me.

"Hi," I said, knowing I didn't have to ask for her to continue whatever story she'd started at the ending.

"I thought I lost my keys at school today. I had to call my mom, and she was pretty annoyed when she showed up. But then we found out I hadn't lost them; I'd only locked them in the car. She was relieved about the keys but still totally annoyed with me. I hope you have something for me to do to keep me out of her hair for the next hour." She fixed me with a very earnest expression.

I would need to think of something. We'd had a surge of volunteers that week. We'd been getting creative to keep them busy. The previous day, Lillian had a pair of teenage boys moving boxes in the storage room that were too heavy for her to lift. The boxes hadn't actually needed to be moved. We hated to turn away kids who wanted to be helpful, whatever their reasons.

Sami was too small to move boxes though. Because she was late, I'd already sent two teenagers away with our last cart of books. I could have her help them, but I already expected it to take less than an hour. Lillian was distracting them to prolong the assignment.

Fortunately, a better idea jumped into my head. "How would you feel about spending an hour reading kids' books?"

"To kids?" Her eyebrows raised in an appearance of self-doubt.

I was surprised by her reaction. I would have guessed that her energetic personality made her a big hit with kids. I shook my head to assure her that wasn't what I meant. "To yourself," I said. "I'm going to start doing some of the storytimes."

Sami smiled. "I still remember coming to storytime with Miss Lillian when I was little. She was *so* funny."

I nodded, trying not to wonder if anyone would remember my reading years from now. My wings would be memorable anyway. "Since it's new for me, I wouldn't mind getting your opinion on some of the books I'm thinking about."

"Really?" She smiled again. It was calmer, almost awed. "My opinion?"

"Yeah. Hang on a second." I hastily printed my list of books, the primary list, not the ones broken into various categories. "Here." I put it on the counter in front of her. "Find as many of these as you can, read them, then mark next to the title how many stars you'd give it as a read-aloud."

"This'll be fun," she said. She grabbed the list, then quickly turned back to me. "Out of five?"

"Yes."

"Yay!" She shook the paper and scampered towards the picture books.

I smiled at her enthusiasm. It wasn't even forced. I could smile again now that I had a plan to apologize. It had been humbling to admit how badly I'd screwed up with Eric. But it had also been necessary. I couldn't be honest with anyone else until I was honest with myself. All the time I was congratulating myself for not letting my attraction to Eric lead me anyplace stupid, I was chasing a different emotion down a rabbit hole just as dark. I didn't just let fear lead, I strapped myself to it. Everything I'd done since I met him had been because I was afraid.

First, I tried to avoid him. He was persistent though, gently persistent. He just kept showing up, trying to get close to me a few words at a time. I wasn't even sure when I started making it easier for him. But for a long time, I'd been trying to prevent him from asking me out not because I was afraid I wouldn't have the guts to say no, but because I was afraid he would stop coming to see me as soon as I did.

The worst part was that I wasn't nearly as blind or ignorant of my emotions as I wanted to pretend. Part of me knew we were forming a bond even without any official declarations. Part of me knew Eric thought he was earning my trust with his patience. I'd somehow convinced myself that if Eric got hurt, he would deserve it for making me afraid in the first place. Not exactly the behavior of a fully rational person I wanted to be. And not the actions of the Christian I was supposed to be.

I knew God would forgive me. That part was easy. I already had Confession scheduled. Eric was another story. All I could do was ask, and that was my plan. It was Friday so I would see him later. I was going to wait for him in the hallway before the meeting. My words were even planned. "Eric, I'm sorry. Can we talk after the meeting?" I would get the apology out, then if he was willing to talk to me, I'd explain and maybe, possibly, see if he might give me another chance.

Because I couldn't help thinking about what Emily had said, or tried to say before her kitchen disaster. She asked what made me rule him out, and I couldn't think of a thing. I liked the qualities he showed in person. I liked the qualities he shared in his lists. I could genuinely say that I liked the person inside that nice package. Fear was the only reason I didn't let myself reevaluate as I got new information. I wasn't going to let fear be a reason anymore. Of course, it was easy to be brave when I was already miserable at the prospect of him never speaking to me again.

I checked out a few books for an older man I didn't recognize except that I knew he'd been in the library before. When he moved aside, Sami rushed the desk. "I didn't get through all of them," she said. "Can you save the rest for me to do tomorrow?"

"You don't usually come in on Saturdays."

"Oh, right." Her eyes darted around. "Tomorrow is Saturday."

"I'll give you another list the next time we get ahead," I said.

She nodded at the offer and began to unfold another sheet of paper. "I remembered my form today." She wasn't laughing at her forgetful nature for a change. It seemed that losing the keys, or perhaps her mom's reaction to the lost keys, had shaken her up. At least for the day. She set the paper on the desk for me to sign.

Lillian came up to cause trouble while I was recording Sami's hour. She asked why we hadn't seen Eric all week.

"Oh!" Sami's expression perked up considerably. "Is he your boyfriend now?"

"No," I said. "Still just friends." I didn't know if even that was true, but I had hope.

Sami managed to frown and wiggle her eyebrows at the same time. "That's too bad." Then she gathered her stuff, all of her stuff, and left.

Lillian wasn't ready to dismiss the topic so easily. She resumed her questioning as soon as we'd waved goodbye to our young helper. "Is he just busy?"

I shrugged because he might also be busy.

She tilted her head to consider me. "You seem down is all. Do you want to talk about what happened?"

It was difficult to resist when she asked in her motherly way. She was concerned, not nosy. Well, perhaps it was a nosy type of concern. It was clear she already knew *something* had happened. I decided to give her a glimpse of the full picture. "I need to apologize," I said, "and then we'll see if he ever comes back."

Lillian didn't press for more information or scold me for doing something that required an apology. She simply nodded and said, "Sounds like you have things well in hand." Then she gave me a stack of books that needed pages taped.

The snow was still hanging around, but it was getting mushy. I noticed that Snowflake had muddy feet when she met me on the porch. I also noticed that she jumped onto my favorite seat on the couch to begin grooming herself. Whatever. It would have time to dry before I had time to sit there. I fed us both, though my appetite was diminished by my nerves. Then I drove to the church.

I got there right as Gabriel, Ruth and Ella arrived to unlock the door. I said hello to them but then hung back as we went down the hall, pretending to check something on my phone. I stayed in the hallway, staring at a prayer on the screen while I listened to the others setting up for our meeting.

I looked up long enough to nod at Isaac and Jessica and smile at adorable Grace. Her eyes were wide, and she actually smiled back. The hallway was quiet long enough that I heard people in the room wondering where everyone was. Eric wasn't there, and I was afraid that was my fault. Sean was missing again, and I couldn't help wondering if that had anything to do with me. Sebastian wasn't there either. I swear I knew nothing about that.

I was about to give up and go in the room when I heard footsteps. I hope Heather couldn't tell I was disappointed. She was clearly *not* disappointed. Her eyes and mouth got big and round as she rushed to catch up to me.

"Julia!" She grabbed my arm in her excitement. "I just talked to Adam."

"Ruth's brother?" I asked.

She rolled her eyes at my ignorance. "Yes, that Adam." She was keeping her voice quiet and glancing towards the open door behind me. "He called me because he heard Kayla was already seeing someone else and wanted to know if that was true. I told him I didn't know because I haven't talked to Kayla in a long time. He asked why so I told him she dumped me about the same time she dumped him. Thank God he didn't ask what we were fighting about. But anyway… do you think that means something!?" Her eyes bore intently into mine.

I didn't even understand the question. "Does what mean something?"

"That he called me! I mean, he could have called one of Kayla's other friends, but he thought of me."

She wanted to know if the phone call meant she had a chance with Adam. The fact that he was asking about Kayla likely meant no one had a chance with him anytime soon. "I… don't know," I said.

Her grip on my arm loosened. "But… maybe?"

"Maybe," I said with a shrug. I didn't want to give her false hope, but I was in the process of demonstrating that I knew less about relationships than I thought. It was a terrible time to ask my advice.

Heather accepted my answer and led me inside. The others must have been waiting for us because I'd barely had time to hang my coat on the back of my chair before we started a prayer.

Then Ruth smiled around the room. "Easy question to start today," she said. "What do these three names have in common?"

"Angels," Isaac said.

"Seriously!?" Ruth glared at her brother as she struggled against a laugh. "I didn't even finish asking the question."

"Oh! Was I right?" He was not trying to hide his laugh or his surprise.

"Yes." Ruth gave an exaggerated sigh. "I was going to say Gabriel, Michael and Raphael."

"How did you do that?" Heather asked.

Isaac shrugged. "Lucky guess."

"No, really," she said. "How did you do that?"

"She said three names and there are only three named angels in the Bible so that was the first thing I thought of," Isaac explained. "There are probably a ton of things you could say three saints have in common, but she said it was easy."

"Okay." Heather looked impressed, then confused. "Hang on. Angels aren't saints. Why do we call them saints?"

Isaac looked at Ruth and Gabriel to see if one of them wanted to explain. It was their topic, after all.

"We call anyone who we believe is in heaven a saint. That's why the good angels get the title," Ruth said. "And why we don't say St. Lucifer."

We did say St. Michael though. Eric liked him. When I remembered that, I felt even worse about him missing the meeting. Was he still so angry that he needed to avoid me? I expected that Eric would at least agree to talk to me, and that I'd spend most of the evening distracted by trying to spot hints on whether or not we'd be able to move forward. Not being able to look for hints was more distracting. I thought I'd at least know one way or the other where I stood, and now I knew nothing. If he no longer sought me out, when and where would I even have a chance to ask for forgiveness?

I tried to follow along with the discussion rather than wallow in sadness. Ruth gloated to her brother the smarty-pants that Lucifer meant there were actually four named angels. He retorted that there were only three who were saints. Ruth said something about how he was still wrong. Then Heather expressed confusion about several points, and Ruth insisted Isaac would explain better.

"So angels can be saints," Heather said slowly, "but saints can't be angels?"

"*People* can't be angels," Isaac said. "Not technically. We sometimes use both terms casually to describe someone who is good, but theologically speaking… God created angels as pure spirits and people with bodies and souls. We don't turn into angels when we're separated from our bodies; they're still a different part of creation."

"But…" Heather had a few more questions.

I tried to listen, but I kept glancing at the door, wondering if Eric was only late. I'd gotten so used to him showing up when I wanted to see him and even when I didn't. He still wasn't there when Emily and Joseph came in, and Heather and Isaac were still going back and forth.

"I guess we should start for real now that everyone's here," Heather said. "Thanks for putting up with my stupidity."

"We're all here to learn," Isaac said.

"Is this everyone?" Joseph asked.

Gabriel shrugged at him.

No one looked at me, thank goodness. I still didn't know anything about Sebastian. And it was flu season. I would point that out if anyone did look at me.

Ruth was looking at Gabriel and pointing at her phone. "Why do I still have this question? I thought we decided not to ask it."

"We did," Gabriel said, "but I don't know why you still have it."

"What's the question?" Joseph asked.

"We're not going to ask it."

He sighed. "Tell me the question then, don't ask me."

Ruth sighed back. "Michael was of course the angel who led the charge against the devil. So we were going to ask where we all thought we could most use his help fighting off the devil today. But that's like asking what sin tempts you the most, and that's way too personal."

"Uh, yeah." Isaac nodded emphatically. "None of us want to go there."

"Which question did we decide to start with?" Ruth asked Gabriel.

He consulted his notebook. Our leadership was not having its most polished week. I was actually happy to see that. Aside from the fact that I wasn't fully engaged myself, I liked that the group was informal.

"I have a question while you guys are figuring things out," Jessica said. She paused, seeking permission to jump into the void.

"Yes, please," Gabriel said.

"I was shopping for baby clothes the other day," she started. "Grace doesn't need anything right now, but sometimes I can't help looking because everything is so cute."

"So cute," Emily repeated.

I smiled my agreement.

"Anyway, I saw this little pink outfit that said 'Mommy's Little Devil' on the front. It had a hood with horns and even a little tail. At first, I thought it was cute, tiny horns and everything. But the more I thought about it, the more it kind of bothered me."

"Bothered you how?" Heather asked.

"Why would I – or anyone else – want to dress my child up like the enemy of God, even in a silly way? It's not the first time I've seen the devil depicted comically, and my question... that I'm trying to put into words… is… When we do that, when we try to make the devil something silly… are we like putting him in his place because he doesn't deserve the respect of angels who chose to obey God… or are we actually giving him more power by not taking him seriously enough?"

"That's deep," Heather said.

"Well…" Joseph pondered the question. "I think it's fair to say our society as a whole treats the devil too lightly. Many don't even believe he exists, and he's convinced an awful lot of people that right and wrong is only a matter of opinion, and not God's opinion. But, on a more personal level, it's harder to say."

"What do you mean by that?" Isaac asked. He sounded curious, not argumentative.

Joseph took a breath and spoke more slowly. "I think if you… or if I… recognize that I'm treating his temptation too lightly, that could be an opportunity to ask for God's help, which is great. But if I'm taking his temptations too seriously, I run the risk of giving in too easily… of admitting defeat to an enemy that is not stronger than God."

"So I think you're saying something like respect the power but not the source," Isaac said.

"Hmm… am I?"

"Uh, guys?" Emily nudged Joseph with her shoulder. "I'm not sure either one of you is talking about horned onesies."

"I did mean it pretty open-ended," Jessica said, "but does anyone have an opinion on the devil baby clothes?"

"Well, Grace would look cute in anything," Heather said.

"I agree." Isaac smiled at his sleeping daughter. "But thank you for not buying it anyway. She already has more clothes than I do."

"That's an exaggeration," Jessica said. "You also don't spit up all over yourself and need to change your clothes three times a day."

"Oh, that's a lovely picture," Ruth said drily. She waved her phone. "We're going to start our questions now."

People nodded. She asked a question loosely related to St. Gabriel. Heather asked Gabriel how he felt about being named after the angel. Gabriel didn't know why his parents chose the name. Then Joseph asked who had seen the new art at the gym because something reminded him of one of the pictures. The meeting continued from there as the most disjointed I'd attended, even not counting me tuning in and out. It also seemed fast.

I was pushing my arms into my coat sleeves when Emily asked me about getting together later. "I talked Ruth and Ella into heading to my place after lunch on Sunday," she said. "And Heather's in, too."

I looked at the women she mentioned, all standing around me. Had I been oblivious to their planning, or had Emily just begun to fill me in? I felt the answer in the way four pairs of eyes picked up that I was asking it. "Uh, okay," I said.

I paid attention long enough to get details. When we split up to leave, I walked out with Heather. She was still obsessing about deeper meaning behind the few sentences she'd exchanged with Adam. It was nice because she didn't expect me to talk, just listen and nod. I was about to get into my car when I felt I needed some time with someone else who didn't expect me to talk.

I walked around the building to the church entrance. Most of the lights were off. It didn't make sense to think of a darker place as a quieter place because those were different senses. I still stepped softly to a pew in the back, sat down slowly to lessen the creaking noise, and set my purse down without letting the strap knock against the back. I exhaled. Then breathed in peace.

Nothing seemed as bad as it had before. It was a small town. I would run into Eric eventually. I would apologize for letting him believe the relationship was going somewhere I intended all along to prevent. I would even be okay if he wasn't willing to try again. Disappointed, yes, but still okay. God was the ultimate comforter.

I'm not sure how long I enjoyed the silence. I was only vaguely aware of a couple other people scattered about until one of then got up and began walking towards the exit. Eric. He was about to pass me. This was my chance. I braced myself to meet his eyes and ask if we could talk.

I saw the moment he recognized me. I was prepared for anger, but there was only sorrow. It crammed the words I prepared down my throat as he smiled against it and continued towards the door. An idea hit me with even more force. I paused only long enough to whisper some gratitude. Then I rushed to my car.

Eric had parked in front of the church. I watched him pulling away from the curb before I started my car. I tried to stay far enough back that he wouldn't notice I was behind him or that I missed my turn. The number was clear on the house, and I repeated it in my head until I got home to write it down.

When I sat down to compose my note, the words came easily.

I'm sorry that I said I didn't want to see you anymore. That isn't true. I'll explain if you want to hear it. Because I know you like lists, I'm making one of reasons you should give me another chance. In no particular order.

- You're supposed to forgive me. It's in the Bible.
- No one enjoys holding a grudge. It's actually in your interest to forgive me.

- I can't keep the fairy wings if we're not friends. I love them and want to keep them.
- You can avoid people asking why you don't go to the library as often.
- No awkwardness on Friday nights.
- You don't say no when someone offers to cook for you. Yes, that's an offer.
- Because I'm ready to admit I want more, too.

I folded up my note, addressed the envelope, drove to the post office, and began to calculate when I might know if Eric accepted my attempt at reconciliation.

16

It was tempting to lie to everyone about Eric, about what had happened between us or didn't happen or... It was tempting. We had barely congregated at Emily's place when Ruth said she could not believe Eric still hadn't made a move even after she sent him to Mrs. Donnelly's with me.

Emily hinted that she might be missing a few puzzle pieces. Heather heard that and demanded details with more details. Ella was the only one with a healthy respect for privacy, though she may have only been too timid to pry.

I wanted to lie because I felt guilty. Guilt was powerful. It had been sticking around underneath the gamut of emotions I'd run through since I last talked to Eric. I'd been remorseful and despairing of any resolution. I'd been elated at the admission that he was actually a promising dating prospect. I'd been angry at myself for being too stubborn to change course as I realized Eric wasn't looking for a doormat. I was more convinced than ever that feelings were a terrible guide. Imagine the confusing mess I'd have made if I'd tried to follow them all at once. After some time to examine the situation with a clear head, I could see that Eric and I were pretty good friends who had a misunderstanding. It was entirely my fault, but I thought he'd probably be willing to work through it.

That vague assessment was what I shared with the group, that we were friends but with some hope. Three of the women were satisfied with vague, though Emily did make me promise to update her if there were any developments. Heather, however, insisted that I stop holding back.

I was, but I wasn't. I wouldn't mind telling them about the note I'd mailed. It didn't make much sense unless I told them about the notes he mailed first, and that didn't feel like my detail to share. Eric addressed them to me and only me. Even if I didn't share the exact contents… they just felt private, between me and him.

I managed to distract Heather with the story of Mrs. Donnelly pouncing when Eric was on her porch, how she trapped him – and me by extension – into a spontaneous volunteer opportunity. Emily continued the new direction and had us in stitches relating the time she'd baked a cake, indirectly, for Mrs. Donnelly and ended up destroying it.

That reminded me of the smoke alarm I'd heard over the phone. She admitted she'd forgotten to remove some packaging on something in the oven. She didn't mind laughing at herself as she described the smell. Also, she wasn't the only one with a story about something not turning out as expected. The afternoon passed quickly.

My evening was quieter, just me and Snowflake and a prayer journal. I filled three pages with gratitude for all the people in my life.

The next morning, I debuted my wings at storytime. I felt silly slipping them on by the desk. The hush as I walked in front of the kids let me know it would be okay. My wings gave me a storytime persona who could relax and put a ton of enthusiasm behind each book.

A little girl came up to me afterwards and asked if they were fairy wings or angel wings. When I asked her what she thought, she whispered, "Angel," in a soft, breathy voice. They could be fairy wings to Eric, angel wings to some of the kids, and plain old confidence for me.

Eric would have been in the back of my mind even if I didn't have his gift tucked in the back room with my coat. But he was safely in the back. I had already obsessed enough to believe I didn't need to obsess yet.

I had mailed my apology letter Friday night, well after the post office had closed. They were closed on Sunday, too. There was no way that operation was efficient enough to get it delivered before Tuesday. That was the earliest I expected to see Eric. All of my attention was on the woman on the other side of the desk when he entered the library late Monday afternoon.

"I think it's supposed to have a white cover," she said.

"Oh, no. Really?" I could hear disappointment in my voice and hoped she understood. The woman – who I guessed to be around my grandmother's age – had come in nearly an hour earlier looking for a book recommended to her by a friend. She couldn't remember the title or author, and we'd had quite a time trying to track it down based on random clues she did remember. I wasn't disappointed because I might have to keep helping her but because I was congratulating myself on finding the proverbial needle in a haystack. Her hesitation interrupted that.

"That's what Evelyn said." She frowned at the book she'd been about to check out.

I frowned at it, too. We might have to start over, unless... "Hey!" I said. "Maybe this is just a different edition. Sometimes the cover changes."

She brightened as I put my hands on my keyboard for a bit of quick research. Research that immediately left my idea unsupported. "Nuts," I muttered. "Looks like all the editions have the same cover."

"Well... you're one of the Chadwick boys, aren't you?"

My head snapped up at the odd question. She wasn't looking at me but off to the side where Eric was leaning against the counter.

He nodded at the older woman. "Yes, ma'am. Eric."

"You the older one or the younger one?"

"Older," he said.

She smiled as though the answer pleased her. "Sorry you've had to wait so long."

I suddenly felt very much out of the loop. How long had she known he was there? How long had be been there? Did he know I was sorry?

"No problem," he said. "Happy to wait my turn."

"I assure you this nice young woman will be worth the wait."

Eric broke into a very short laugh, which he settled into a pleasant smile. What was that all about? He did seem to be in a good mood. That was something. I was about to tell him I'd be with him as soon as I could to put on a front of professionalism.

My charge beat me to it. She said to both of us, "Why don't we ask if he just has a quick question?"

"I was hoping Julia might have some volunteer work for me today," he said.

"Oh, I... I just gave someone the last cart of books to be put away," I said. I could probably find something for him to do, but not without a significant interruption for the person I was already helping. That front of professionalism needed support.

Fortunately, I was not the only employee. Lillian appeared out of nowhere. "Oh, I have a job for him." She pointed at Eric, then wiggled her finger for him to follow as she walked away from the desk.

He gave a polite nod before he went after Lillian as though helping her was the only reason he was at the library.

I paused a moment to hope helping Lillian wasn't the only

reason he was at the library. Then I turned my focus on recapping the mystery. "Okay," I said. "A book on church history. Probably not Hahn or Pitre or—"

"You know what, I'll just take this one," she interrupted, shoving the book across the desk towards me.

"Uh…" I was taken aback by the only definitive sentence she'd uttered since she'd asked me for help. "You want this one?"

"That young Mr. Chadwick – I've already forgotten his first name – seems like a nice guy."

"He is," I said with a nod.

"I'll take this one." She tapped the book then gave a significant glance the direction Eric went as though he had something to do with her decision.

I gave a mental shrug and scanned her library card. When her name appeared on my screen, I saw that her last name was Jones. I was about to ask if she was related to Sebastian when I realized that her last name was *Jones*. Even in a small town, it felt foolish to ask if she happened to be related to someone else with one of the most common last names ever. I simply checked out her book and slid it back across the counter. "Come back if you find out it's not the right one."

"Thanks, dear." She smiled at me. "If you see Evelyn coming in for a copy of this one, you'll know I liked it."

I nodded and waved as she moved away, though I still didn't have a clue who Evelyn was, other than the woman she kept blaming for not giving her enough information.

I was curious what sort of job Lillian had for Eric, but I figured he'd come back by the desk eventually. It was by the exit. I scanned in some books that were returned while I was helping Ms. Jones and lined them up on a little cart. I was shifting some paperwork when I heard Lillian's voice. She was leading Eric around a corner. She looked at me and waved him towards the front desk. Eric was carrying a stack of at least a dozen fairly thick books.

"Stand there for one minute," she instructed. Then she pulled the books from his stack one at a time. She examined each cover before setting two of the books aside and putting the rest on the same cart I'd just partially filled.

I had no idea what she was doing, but I wasn't going to question my boss's sanity. Plus, I was trying to pretend I was paying more attention to my work than to the unresolved tension between me and Eric. Was he there to see me or was he just being a mature person who didn't stop volunteering because I rejected him?

"Great." Lillian nodded with satisfaction when she got through the books. She pushed the cart towards Eric. "Now you can put these away."

He nodded at her with a strange expression. He didn't argue at all before heading back to nonfiction. I had barely finished not watching him walk away when Lillian nudged me aside. "I'll do this," she said. "You go see if he needs any help."

Now I knew what she was doing. "Thanks," I said.

She smiled and nodded after Eric.

I found him laughing to himself. Fingers of doubt began to strangle my hope. Did he expect me to follow him, and was that funny? "What's up?" I asked as casually as I could.

"Oh, um..." He bit the side of his lip, looking embarrassed at having been caught laughing.

I chose to interpret the reaction to mean he had not been expecting me and was therefore not laughing at me. A perfect example of logic overruling feelings.

"She just pulled these books off the shelves," he said. "I'm probably crazy because it looked like she knew what she was doing, but for some reason I felt like she was making stuff up as she went."

"Huh." That was all I said. If we explored his suspicions, I would end up lying or admitting my boss had just orchestrated an opportunity for me to talk to him. Far better to take advantage of the opportunity than to dwell on how it happened. And if we were going to talk, we were really going to talk. "Did you get my note?"

"Yeah." He pulled back the book he'd been about to fit onto a shelf. "That's why I'm here. Obviously."

There was something about the way he said that last word that made me laugh and get defensive at the same time. "It's not that obvious. I didn't mail it until very late on Friday and..."

Eric was staring at the book in his hands. When I mailed the letter wasn't as important as why.

"Do you forgive me?" I asked, rather timidly.

"I don't think... It's not a sin to say no to someone you don't want to spend time with." He didn't look up, and I swear he was holding his breath.

"It is if I made you think I... but I was hoping to keep... I wasn't honest about..." Instead of continuing to babble, I cut to the point and said, "You scare me."

That got his attention. He looked confused as he stepped around the little cart to put it between us.

"I don't mean..." Neither of us wanted to talk about past relationships, but it was important that he understood where I was coming from. "The last time I dated someone, I tried so hard to be what he wanted, I stopped being me. I'm afraid of doing that again."

Eric actually nodded as though he was glad I told him that. "Do you think you're doing it now?"

"Doing what?"

"Have you been trying to... not be yourself around me?"

I shook my head. If anything, I'd been trying to reveal more of me so I'd know right away if something drove him away.

"Okay," Eric said. "We're off to a good start because I already know I like you." He finally slid the book onto the shelf. "I really like you."

Now I was really blushing. Warm, incoherent thoughts flooded my head, trying to drown the feeling of being admired by a nice and, yes, very cute guy.

"Even when we disagree," he said.

"We, uh, haven't really disagreed about anything. At least, before now."

He laughed and turned indignant eyes on me. "You called hockey stupid."

"When did I say that?"

"I don't know. Maybe two months ago." He gave me a playful glare. "You said it was a bunch of guys skating around between fights. You also implied that I might be leaking brain cells every time I watched a game."

"That... seems like a pretty specific thing to *imply*," I said.

He sighed at me. "And you don't even remember."

I smiled fully at his banter. The friendship was resurrecting but with it was the knowledge that it wasn't where either of us wanted to stay. We were trying to move forward and backward at the same time. We needed to move out of the library. Meeting somewhere else would prove I was ready to leave my comfort zone. The problem wasn't fear. But there was still a problem. I wanted him to be the one to ask me, and he already had. Could I word it like I was accepting late, or did his invitation not count because I vetoed it once? "I should at least pretend to be working," I said. "Maybe we could plan to talk more later?"

Eric nodded, but he didn't say anything. I couldn't tell that he was waiting for me. He seemed satisfied to talk at some unspecified later. Well, I wasn't satisfied. I was trying to prove I was no longer afraid, and I wanted to prove it right now. "Since I don't have to work on Wednesday, I'll have plenty of time to make a nice dinner," I hinted.

He only nodded again.

"And you know where I live." I finally felt brave enough to meet his eyes.

They were practically dancing with amusement. "Are you offering to make me dinner?"

"I'm trying to make it okay for you to ask me to."

"It's not okay for me to invite myself over just because you make it tempting."

I sighed because it had become clear he was being difficult on purpose. "Will you still ask me if I make it tempting enough?" I was trying to think of things he had said he liked to eat.

That might not have been where his mind was. His mouth opened without words and bits of color creeped up his neck.

I kept thinking about food.

Eventually, he shook off the stupor and said, "Will you agree to have dinner with me if I let you pick the place?"

I smiled at the compromise. "Okay. Come over any time after work."

"And maybe we can finally exchange numbers?"

I said okay to that, too. We said an easy goodbye since it was really a see you soon.

I passed a Valentine display Lillian and I had set up about two weeks earlier as I hurried back to the front desk. I'd passed it so many times I didn't pay attention to it anymore except there was a thought buried in my head that we would need to take it down soon. But that thought tunneled over to a few other thoughts and made me hunt down a calendar. I needed to call Emily as soon as I got home.

17

"Hi, Julia. What's up?" Emily's perky voice came through my phone.

"I have good news and bad news."

"Which one is the problem?"

"Both," I said.

"Interesting," she said with a laugh.

Evidently, my tone made it clear that it wasn't a serious problem. It was already Wednesday morning. She'd been at work when I got home on Monday and her battery had died. We swapped a few texts on Tuesday to set up a time to talk. I knew she was going to tell me it wasn't a big deal, but I wanted to hear in her voice that she meant it.

"I just need some advice," I said.

"Okay. I can do advice as long as I don't have to promise it'll be good advice."

That made me laugh. But I was in a good mood so it didn't take much. "I talked to Eric on Monday and got everything smoothed over between us."

"Yay! I'm guessing that's the good news."

"Yes," I said. "It's very good."

"Yay, yay, yay! And when you say good, does that mean you two are officially together now?"

"Uh… well, I don't know how official anything is, but he is coming over for dinner tonight."

Emily gasped. "You have a Valentine's Day date? That is…"

"The problem," I finished for her.

"What? Wait." She was laughing too hard to talk, and I knew she was laughing at me, but I could take it. I heard her suck in a calming breath. "*Why* is that a problem?" she asked.

"Because I didn't know it was Valentine's Day."

"When?"

"When we planned to get together."

"Uh…" Emily paused. "You said you just talked to him on Monday. That was two days ago. You didn't know Valentine's Day was in two days?"

"No. You know I think sappiness is silly. I've probably been blocking out mentions of it."

"Okay," Emily said. "I still don't get why it's a problem though."

"What if he doesn't know that I didn't know? What if he thinks I picked Valentine's Day on purpose and am expecting… some elaborate… whatever?"

"Uh."

There was enough thoughtfulness in the syllable that I could tell I'd convinced Emily of something. I waited to see if advice was coming.

"I guess my advice would be to just tell him you're not expecting a big elaborate whatever."

"Just tell him?" I asked.

"Yeah."

"What if he doesn't even realize what day it is and thinks me bringing it up is some sort of hint?"

"Unlikely," she said. "Even if he didn't realize it when you made plans, he'll be at work all day today, right? Someone will say something about Valentine's Day before dinner."

"A simple message will make everything fine?"

"I think so," Emily said. "He'll probably be relieved to hear it. I think some guys get a little stressed out about the expectations. Joseph made me tell him exactly what I wanted. He said, 'Please don't make me guess because it will end badly for both of us.'"

I laughed again. "What are you two doing anyway?"

"Well, we both have to work. I'm going to stop at the gym during his lunch break, and he's going to give me a card."

"A card?"

"Yeah. I told him he had to make me a card," Emily said. "Just a couple of sentences of mushy thoughts, and I'll be happy."

"Wow. You told him exactly what you wanted and still didn't make it easy."

"What?"

"I doubt he's excited about writing down mushy thoughts."

"Hmm," Emily said. "Maybe. But easier to write than to say."

I thought of the notes Eric and I exchanged and smiled. "You might have a point."

"Of course I do. Do you need any more advice?"

"No. I think I have dinner covered."

Emily laughed. "The only advice I'd have on cooking is to make sure your smoke alarm is working, and you probably don't need that."

"I hope not," I said.

She laughed again and told me she was glad she had so far avoided any major cooking disasters at work. Chip kept her focused. He also kept her entertained. She told me about her favorite customer, a police officer who growled right back at Chip. Emily made the pair sound funny, but I thought they'd be scary in person.

I thought Chip was a lot scarier than she did.

By the time we hung up, I was completely rational again about the whole Valentine's Day thing. I simply sent Eric a text that said I noticed the date and wanted to be sure he knew I wasn't expecting anything special because of it. He replied that he was looking forward to dinner and that I could expect him by six.

I was going to make lasagna with some fresh baked bread. I wasn't sure if that was traditional or cliché, but I knew he said he liked it at some point. The bread was my primary objective. If I spent the afternoon baking bread, my house would smell good. I didn't think Snowflake was a stinky cat, but if my house smelled like litter box, I was probably around it too much to notice. Bread was better.

The bread was on the counter, and I was literally standing in front of it basking in the aroma when the doorbell rang. I looked down as I opened the door because Snowflake zoomed through. I wondered for a second if she thought it was strange for someone else to be on the porch at my usual time. She probably didn't care as long as I let her in. Then I looked at Eric, who was holding flowers.

I didn't know what to say so I just stepped back to let him follow Snowflake. I closed the door before I turned back.

He could tell I was staring at the purple and white flowers. His eyes moved from them to me uncertainly as he handed them to me. "I, uh, hope you like these."

"They're nice," I said. I held them to my nose. "They smell nice, too."

He closed his eyes, almost wincing. "But?" he prompted.

"Well, I... you got my message, right?"

"Yeah?"

I looked at the flowers again. "Where I said you didn't have to..."

He shook his head at me, looking a little exasperated. "You've been pretty clear about not being interested in any emotional drivel and when you didn't even mention that it was going to be Valentine's Day, I thought that confirmed that you wanted to treat it like any other day. But then you sent me a message about not wanting anything special. Nothing special is not nothing. It's *something*." He gestured helplessly at the flowers. "I tried."

I put the flowers back to my nose to appear more appreciative. It wasn't the scent that made me smile though. It was what he said. Eric cared what I wanted. That was more proof that he wanted me to be me. Even if he got it wrong, the fact that he cared was the best gift. There was also a chance I was partly to blame for the crossed wires. "Thank you," I said.

He looked relieved that I sounded sincere.

Neither of us moved for a moment. He was probably just waiting for me to invite him farther inside. I was consumed by an uninvited image in my head. It seemed like a perfect moment for Eric to kiss me. Not some anxiety-riddled first kiss, but a sweet moment that an established couple might share. Was there any way we could skip ahead to something like that? Now that I was thinking that we were not at my place of employment and there was a very real chance he might try to kiss me at some point, I kind of wanted to get it over with so I could stop wondering when.

I willed those thoughts aside and motioned for him to follow me into the kitchen. "You can throw your coat anywhere," I said as I started opening cupboards. I was pretty sure I didn't own a vase. I didn't know what I was looking for, just something that would hold flowers.

"It smells wonderful in here," Eric said.

"Glad you approve," I said. "And thank you." A compliment could be an opening for a kiss, too. I so needed to stop thinking about that. I pulled out a plastic pitcher. It would not make the most attractive display. But I could put water in it, and it was tall enough that the flowers wouldn't tip it over. I set them on the counter rather than the table so we'd have room for food.

Also, there was already a game on the table. I walked over to it and pulled the lid off the box. "I borrowed this from Emily," I said. She'd dropped it off on her way to work. "And she actually borrowed it from Joseph's parents and… Anyway, it just has a bunch of, like, get to know people questions."

Eric nodded as he pulled out a card to examine. "It's time to start talking about *important things*?"

"Why do you say it like that?" I asked. "It sounds like you're mocking me."

"Oh, no. No." He held his hands out in a show of innocence. "I think you're absolutely right that people should talk about things that matter, make sure they're on the same page from the beginning when it might be easier to… It's just… you say important things like some people might say deal-breakers so you can't blame me for worrying that…" He lowered his hands to the table, a slightly defeated expression passing across his face.

"I know," I said, because I did know. It was already too late for either of us to escape the relationship unharmed. That was my fault. My fear of growing close had prevented the deeper conversations. And yet, not entirely. Eric's notes had fed me bits of valuable information when I thought I wasn't ready. His patience had teased out details beneath the surface as well. We actually knew each other fairly well despite my attempts at sabotage. I had reason to hope.

But darn it, we couldn't talk about important things when every thought that crossed my mind ended with a kiss. We really needed to address the elephant in my head.

Eric picked up another card and continued reading questions to himself. His eyebrows came together. "This asks what color best defines the mood I'm in right now? What does that mean?"

I just shook my head and said, "We're not going to answer stupid questions."

"Thank you." He put that card down and picked up a different one. "Oh!" His eyes widened a moment later. "How did storytime go on Monday?"

"I don't think that's on the card," I said.

He smiled. "No. It says something about a talent you wish more people recognized. That reminded me of your talent for storytime and that I forgot to ask about it."

"I think it went well."

"Did you wear the wings?"

"Oh, yeah. They were a big hit."

"I knew you'd be a beautiful fairy." His eyes went back to the card.

I couldn't even concentrate enough to read the card right in front of me. If Eric could make up his own question, then so could I. I took a deep breath. "Are you planning to kiss me tonight?"

Every muscle in his face froze. His eyes lifted to mine very slowly before he said, "I don't think that's on a card either."

"You started it."

"I didn't know we weren't allowed to..." He couldn't seem to finish the sentence, to continue to run away from my question. "*Planning* is not the word I would use."

I nodded that I understood. Planning, at least the way I said it, did have some shifty undertones. I tried to explain myself. Badly. "I'm sorry," I said. "I'm distracted with wondering and thought maybe we could get it over with so I can think about something else."

Eric's expression went from uncomfortable to somewhat offended.

"I didn't mean that," I said quickly. "I didn't mean get it over with like... I meant this nervous awkwardness that I'm feeling about it. I would like to get that over with, instead of making it worse by talking about it." I looked back at the card in a desperate attempt to redirect.

He continued to stare at me as though there was no possible way to respond. I could feel the stare.

My feelings were being stupid again. I was trying to turn a tender moment into something logical. There was nothing logical about wanting to smash faces with someone. The timer on my oven started beeping. Saved by the bell, a cliché I totally loved at the moment.

I intended to take the lasagna out of the oven and let it cool for a while so we could try some questions that were actually from the cards. Eric followed me though.

"Can I help?" he asked.

I nodded and pointed. "Plates are in there."

He got out two plates and found some glasses while I sliced the bread. He asked if he could put the lasagna on the table for me. I got out a serving spoon. By the time we got everything on the table, I was more distracted than ever by all the waxing and waning of his proximity.

"I think... um... Are you ready to eat?" I was looking at the table, trying to make sure we had everything.

Eric was behind me. I felt his hand slide into mine and pull just enough to turn me around to face him.

"We can get it over with if that's what you want," he said, "but I don't think it's going to help me think about anything else."

My heart told me not to move, and for once I thought the most intelligent thing I could do was listen.

"Julia?"

Getting my attention was unnecessary since I was right in front of his face and struck once again by how incredibly blue his eyes were. I thought he must be looking for confirmation that it was still what I wanted. I took a tiny step closer.

"Is this..." He cleared his throat and tried again. "Is this one of the important things? Are you going to kick me out if I do it wrong?"

My forehead fell against his chest as I burst out laughing. I couldn't help it. The idea of kicking him out was so ridiculous when I didn't even want to let go of his hand.

I felt him exhale against my hair. "Feeling a little less tension now, are we?"

I nodded and got control of myself. As soon as I looked up again, he kissed me. He kissed me more than once actually. Each time I became more convinced that my feelings were not the enemy of my thoughts. Like faith and reason, the two could work together if I let them. Eric let go of my hand to suggest I sit first, then he joined me at the table. We prayed together and enjoyed the meal I'd prepared with a side of important things. Eric liked me even though I made a lot of mistakes. I liked him even though I thought I didn't want to. The more we learned about each other, the more those feelings began to make sense.

www.ingramcontent.com/pod-product-compliance
Lightning Source LLC
Chambersburg PA
CBHW031341170626
46807CB00002B/783